Simply Fate

Mark J. Graham

First Edition 2022

ISBN-13: 978-1-913822-30-9

Dedications

This book, and the beginning of my writing journey, is dedicated to my whole family.

"This time next year Rodders..."

Acknowledgements

This journey has been one of many twists and turns and the people I would like to thank are too many to mention here. But especially to my agent and sounding board, Ken Scott for helping a local lad become an actual author.

To my family and friends who have read many varying versions of this story, my wife Helen for allowing me to be a whirlwind entrepreneur, never questioning my sometimes-questionable antics. To my proud parents for never faltering in their belief that this would become a reality and everyone close to me who has promised to buy their own copy and support my journey.

I thank you all from the bottom of my heart.

Finally to my two sons, Alex & Aaron.

Follow your passion. Follow your dreams.

In a world filled with endless possibilities, you can do whatever you want to do and never follow the status quo.

1

The World Lottery

'Can you believe some lucky son of a bitch won the lottery rollover?' Tom moaned. 'It's all over the bloody papers.'

He was reading the local Daily Chronicle at our small lounge table as Simon and I were settling into our first pint of beer in preparation for the region's biggest football match for years.

'Yeah and they're from the UK, the lucky bastards,' Simon said as he gulped down his beer. 'I didn't have a single number and some fluky git matched all eight? You must be the luckiest prick on the planet to do that.'

'Then, to top it all off, they're the only winner!' Tom said, flipping to another story and tearing the page in frustration.

I took a mouthful of ice-cold myself. I pondered the thought for a moment as the national news channel summarised a report on the severe weather around the country on the TV.

The snow had battered the UK for the last month and was still causing chaos. The pretty blonde reporter was braving the appalling weather outside the UK Lottery Headquarters in London, the snow whipping into her face as she spoke into the microphone. 'With a winning total of over two hundred and forty-five million Pounds, this unprecedented jackpot will make someone exceptionally wealthy. But our sources inside lottery HQ tell us that, as of right now, the winner has not claimed the biggest single winning jackpot in lottery history. The only new information we have is that the winning ticket was purchased somewhere in the northeast of England.' She signed off. 'Katie Bell, News 24, outside a rather chilly London Lottery Headquarters.'

'Holy shit, it's someone on our doorstep,' said Tom. 'I can't believe the sad bastard doesn't even know they've won!'

'Well it certainly wasn't any of us. We wouldn't be sitting here drinking this watered down piss would we?' Si replied.

The World Lottery was a fairly new and unique draw which involved twenty countries from around the world. The winners only had six days to claim the jackpot, or it would be rolled over to the next week's draw. The current jackpot had rolled over for a record nine weeks.

The media was in a frenzy, loving the fact that time was almost up for the potential winning and unclaimed jackpot ticket.

The local sports bar was jammed to the rafters with Geordies wearing the usual black-and-white striped shirts to prepare for their beloved Newcastle United to line up against bitter local rivals Sunderland.

It was the FA Cup, and we had been drawn together in the fifth round. Sunderland hadn't been around the Premier League for some years now, languishing in the third tier of English football, playing the likes of Accrington Stanley and Burton Albion while we faced the likes of Chelsea, Man United, Liverpool and Arsenal.

The bar was a mecca for Newcastle football fans. Three floors of bars, pool tables and wide-screen TVs, televising every sporting event imaginable. A sports fanatic's paradise, which was currently filled with a sea of support for the home team.

Although Newcastle upon Tyne and Sunderland are merely a few miles apart, the rivalry when it comes to sport was one of embroiled passion and, in some instances akin to a war. The fixture was always so much more than just a game.

As I gazed up at one of the huge flat screens, a light bulb flashed in my head as I'd realised that after all this time, I hadn't checked my lottery ticket either. Why the hell hadn't I checked it at my parents' house this morning? I cursed myself quietly. My heart beat a little faster as my imagination began to run riot.

I rummaged inside my pockets, placed the contents onto the table next to my drink. I found a few 20 pound notes and the hand-written lottery slip that I completed every week.

'You lost something big, lad?' asked Tom.

'Just making sure I picked up my wallet,' I lied. I was now slightly concerned that my ticket was not with the completed lottery slip, as it usually was.

'That old chestnut,' he replied, heading off to the bar.

'Lend me that paper a second, Si?' I said.

I scrolled through the pages to the lottery results and found the winning numbers in a segment dedicated to what the actual jackpot could purchase. There were pictures of private jets, top of the range sports cars and hugely expensive houses.

To win the jackpot, you had to select eight numbers in total. They were there at the top of the page in bold typeface: 4, 8, 16, 19, 27, 44. Then, two special numbers drawn from a separate lottery machine: 2 and 9.

I studied the numbers carefully, instantly aware of the fact that the same regular numbers I played each week were not the winning numbers. And yet I had also played a line of 'lucky dip' numbers and didn't have a clue what those numbers were.

For as long as I can recall, my infatuation with winning the lottery has been slightly unhealthy. My reputation as a daydreamer precedes me and I tend to live more in my own world, than in the real one.

I'd opted for voluntary redundancy the previous month from the large telecoms company I'd been employed with for nearly six years. Having more time on my hands had only intensified my imagination.

Everyone said I was mad to take redundancy, but the reality was that there was no buzz or excitement there. The job was boring and while I was effective in my role, nothing compared to the excitement of the military.

I had joined the Royal Marines at aged 17, spent ten years as a 'Bootneck' and loved every second, even during my two stints in Afghanistan. Ten years and honourably discharged after 'the incident'.

My obsession with luxury and a lottery win probably stemmed from the memories of the rather poor neighbourhood I grew up in. Whilst we didn't have much, it was a great place to live. I had a loving family and a tight-knit circle of friends. My parents worked hard just to survive and pay bills, so luxury was always another world away.

My two younger brothers and I were always priority in the eyes of our parents and they would try hard to give us the best in life. However, that was difficult, living on only one wage from my father. The local postman's salary was not fantastic and maybe deep down I wanted better for my family and would love to pay them back for all the sacrifices they made for us all.

Maybe if I was a multi-millionaire, I would eventually pluck up the courage and ask out Tom's sister, Erika. A vision of beauty and the sexiest woman I have ever laid my eyes on. I'd never found the courage or the right time to ask her out on a date. My lack of confidence with women stemmed from my youth, extremely over-weight and somewhat of a recluse outside of my small circle of friends.

Bullying was a major part of my life throughout school. From name-calling to beatings, I experienced the worst side of what school life had to offer. My family and very few friends I had, had no idea what I experienced and rather than confront it, I merely buried its existence and continued to eat more food for comfort, hence making the situation worse. I spent a lot of time in my own company and dealt with things privately, in my own way.

My home life was a saving grace. If I'd not had such a loving family, I fear my fate would have taken a far different route. It was only when I knew I wanted to join the Marines that I realised I had to get fit. I started taking care of myself, eat healthily, and hit the gym on a daily basis, all the while wondering when I would have the confidence in my appearance to ask Erika out.

I knew what it took to pass the Royal Marine selection course and to complete basic training. These soldiers were the toughest in the world. The 30-mile hike across Dartmoor in full kit, which had to be completed in under seven hours, was devised by the devil himself. It broke the toughest of men.

Erika was the perfect woman in my eyes and although I've wanted so much to just ask her out on a date, my courage went every time I got anywhere near her. She was completely in the dark about how I felt about her.

Could becoming instantly wealthy buy some much needed confidence? Probably not.

In the back of my mind, I knew I still had a second lucky dip line on my lottery ticket, so maybe I stood a slim chance. But with odds of around one hundred and twenty million to one, who was I kidding?

Tom returned with our drinks and the TV volume was cranked up. We clinked glasses and the match eventually kicked off to a deafening roar. Any lingering thoughts of vast wealth disintegrated into my pint glass.

2

'It can't be ... it's not possible.'

'And finally,' sang the local brunette newsreader, a false smile perched on her face, 'to recap our main news this morning; the world's largest lottery jackpot prize, a record breaking two hundred and forty-five million pounds, still remains unclaimed. The lucky individual is currently losing a colossal thirty-thousand pounds per day in interest ... and has only two days left to claim the jackpot.'

Then a heart-stopping moment as she said, 'Furthermore, sources at Lottery HQ have this morning revealed that the winning ticket was purchased right here in Newcastle upon Tyne.'

It had been a great day. The humiliating thrashing of our local rival was a moment to be savoured and celebrated to the maximum, but the hangover that followed was a reminder that when it came to drinking, I was a bit of a lightweight.

The reporter's words quickly reminded me that I was still to check my lucky dip lottery ticket. 'Shit.' My whole body was frozen to the spot for a moment. My heart was racing powerfully as I was hit with nervous panic.

I managed to prise myself from the sofa, narrowly avoiding the half-eaten pizza that lay in the open box on the floor. I hurried to the small bag of clothes dumped near the door from the trip to my parent's house a few days ago; the bag was split open and half the damp clothes were lying strewn on the floor. I swiftly rummaged through the pile until I found the jeans I'd been wearing when I purchased the ticket.

'Thank God,' I whispered, pulling them a little closer to my chest. I checked the first pocket, then the second, third and fourth. Each one was empty. I panicked a little, peeling one piece of clothing after another from the remaining pile.

I repeated the process three or four times, each one more frantic than the last. I searched through the entire bag and every item of clothing. Nothing.

Trying to stay calm, I searched my hung-over memory as to what had happened since I purchased the ticket. My headache was intensely magnified, my heart still racing as sweat from my brow began to roll down my face. The small front room was beginning to feel like an overheated sauna as my stress levels increased with every breath. Where the hell did I put the ticket?

I started pacing around my small coffee table in the lounge, rubbing my cheeks with both hands and repeating the same words over and over, 'Think, Mark think, think.' I retraced the steps I'd taken when I entered the flat the day before. I had spent the full day at home after visiting my parents and then yesterday had gone to the pub which is when I discovered the ticket was missing.

'Shit.' I searched the rest of the flat, my bedroom, kitchen, bathroom, dining area and in every corner and every unit. Unable to remain still and feeling desperate, my panic turned to anger. I pulled all the cushions from the sofa and checked down the back and sides. I searched every nook and cranny but found nothing.

Slumping back onto the sofa, the cushions now scattered all over my living room floor, I inhaled hard, as I frantically tried to keep things together. I'm panicking for no reason, I thought, exhaling loudly. People like me don't win the lottery. We dream about it, yes. But win? Surely not, that's just the way it is with normal people. The ticket may have been purchased in my city, but I need to be realistic here, right?

Closing my eyes and trying to stay focused, I visualised the day I purchased the ticket moment by moment, trying to replay and retrace my steps from when I'd actually visited the store.

I recalled that after I'd left the small newsagents with my ticket tucked casually into my rear pocket, I'd walked the short distance to my parent's house using my usual route. I struggled through the snow and freezing winds. The weather in the region had taken a turn for the worst over the last few days, blizzards and icy chills had launched the country into a panic and with only seven days to go until December 25th, we would unquestionably experience the region's first white Christmas in decades.

I stayed the night at my parents' house, only leaving the four walls to have a snowball fight with my two younger brothers in the back garden. I'd removed my wet clothes, placed them into a black bag, and left them in the laundry room overnight.

The next day I'd struggled home through the thick snow, hopping into bed pretty early as I wanted to have a clear head for 'match day'.

There was only one thing for it. I would physically walk the route I'd taken and check to see if the ticket had fallen from my pocket at any point of my journey. But who was I kidding? The snow was at least two or three feet deep in most areas and the flakes had dropped incessantly from the sky for the last sixteen days straight. Any ticket that may have fallen on the route from any of these places, would surely now be buried within the substantial white layers. And besides, should I really go to all this trouble, when I couldn't actually be certain if my ticket was a winner?

Catching myself in the mirror, I stared blankly at my reflection. Certainly not an ugly chap by any means, but my face had aged somewhat with my unlucky genetics, coupled with the stress levels I'd endured during my six long, boring years in the telecoms business.

In the kitchen I opened the morning newspaper as I swallowed two painkillers … and I almost choked. The front page hit me like a bullet to the head: Winning Ticket Purchased Here read the large, bold headline. A photograph of a shabby-looking newsagent was published directly underneath and I instantly recognised the entrance of the store. I dropped the paper to the floor. 'It can't be … it's not possible.'

When I finally caught my breath, I pulled open the kitchen drawer. 'Okay, let's calm down and think.' I got a pen and notepad from the drawer and sat down on the sofa. The only thing left to do now was make a list of my exact steps.

I had to admit it was liable to be a worthless, impossible task which would no doubt end in disappointment, even if I miraculously found my ticket. But I had to at least try.

3

Hope Fading Fast

Without showering and still wearing the same clothes from yesterday, I grabbed my long winter coat and woollen gloves and hurried out the front door.

My apartment was on the fourth floor of a large apartment block. I slowly made my way down each flight of stairs, exploring every step carefully until I reached the bottom, finding nothing but a half empty bottle of fizzy drink and several cigarette butts.

Opening the door of the apartment block, the major problem hit me as hard as the icy breeze outside. There was heavy, thick snow as far as the eye could see, completely covering the cars, buildings, and pavements. If the ticket had fallen from my pocket at any point whilst walking, it would surely be buried and impossible to find.

But that wasn't going to stop me, because it was just possible that a small section of the ticket would protrude from the snow and if anyone was going to find it, it would be me. The lottery ticket was a bright shade of red and should be easy to spot.

With my eyes glued to the snow-covered pavement in front of me, I walked slowly but purposefully towards the local store.

I arrived at the grocery store empty-handed and disillusioned. The store itself was relatively small, with only three small aisles for shopping. I picked up a small carry basket and walked casually up the first aisle.

The floor was soaking wet from previous visitors and a shop attendant was aimlessly mopping the floor just ahead of me. 'What the hell am I doing?' I asked myself as I scanned the floor. They would have cleaned the floor continuously with all the snow. I have no chance of finding anything here.

But still I searched, the frustration building up as I quickly turned at the top aisle and continued down the second. The floor was fresh from the attendant's mop, and the only way I would find anything lost in the store was to ask an assistant for help. But why would a lottery ticket, discarded on the floor with the melted snow and dirt, be handed in as lost property? I was crazy to even think that would ever happen, especially a ticket potentially worth two hundred and forty-five million Pounds.

Arriving at the third aisle, I picked up a sports drink and a chocolate bar, my ultimate hangover cure and headed to the assistant at the checkout.

'Would someone be able to check your lost property for me, do you think?' I asked her.

'Sure, what have you lost?'

'A visa card, 20 quid cash, and a lottery ticket.'

She raised an eyebrow at me. 'A lottery ticket?'

'Yes.'

She laughed. 'Like anyone is going to hand that in.'

I knew she was right. Why was I even bothering going through the motions? I paid for my goods and she handed me my change from the till, asking me to wait a few moments.

I paced the wet floor, checking my watch every ten seconds for what seemed like an eternity. A few minutes later, she returned and predictably confirmed that I was out of luck.

'Of course, but thanks anyway.' I made my way out of the store and back into the biting arctic winds.

My stress levels were beginning to boil over as I continued to meander up the icy street, frustratingly digging up the snow with my feet. 'Shit … shit!' I cried, kicking up a large patch of snow, stopping an elderly couple in their tracks on the opposite side of the road.

And then, a brainwave. Might the ticket have fallen into my parents' garden?

Inspecting the streets seemed pointless and as I approached my parents' street, apart from feeling frozen from the icy wind chills, I was already beginning to admit to myself that I'd probably lost the ticket for good.

As I entered their street, I my pace reduced to a gentle stroll, allowing my heart rate to slow down so I could catch my breath. Stopping at the gate, I glanced up to the sky and chanted a small prayer to myself.

My parents lived in a simple, incredibly dated terraced property, just on the edge of town. Housing its original, ancient features of exposed beams and dated décor, you get a sense of history every time you enter the place. I still fall in love with the charm it holds, even after all this time.

I trudged down the small pathway towards the front door, scanning the ground in front of me. The quaint garden was unscathed, lying in at least three feet of snow. I kicked it up sporadically, before taking a deep breath and entering to find my mother ironing my dad's shirts in the hallway.

'Hi son, what are you doing here?' she asked, cruising the iron across the shirt sleeve.

'Do I need an excuse to pop round for a coffee and see my parents?' I replied as she glanced at me, raising an inquisitive eyebrow. She knew I was up to something.

'Okay, okay,' I added, 'I lost something the other day and I've come around to have a look. Is that a crime?'

'Well, what have you lost?' she asked, heading into the kitchen to fill the kettle. 'Coffee?'

'Yeah, that would be great,' I replied. 'I lost my bank card and a lottery ticket. Have you seen them?'

I tried to keep my tone casual, trying not to show my anxiety, but deep down I wanted to run through the house yanking at every piece of bloody furniture.

'No,' she called out, 'I've not found anything.'

'I'm gonna look in the back garden.' I felt somewhat deflated, but still held onto a tiny flicker of hope. She brought me a coffee, and I took a mouthful as I headed out to the garden at the rear of the house.

My dad kept a small storage area for his tools at the entrance to the garden. I pulled out one of his old garden spades, made my way to the garden and contemplated the task ahead. The area was approximately 40 feet squared; pretty basic with very little flower bed and a small, grassed area, currently sitting three feet under snow.

Starting from the far right corner, I vigorously dug into the snow, lifted the spade maybe two feet high, then slowly allowed the white flakes to filter back to the ground. I continued in one straight line, repeating the process when I reached the top of the garden.

I found nothing but snow and lumps of ice. Making a second and third line with the old spade, I continued digging and sifting through the thick snow, but when I finished there was still no ticket in hand. I hurled the spade full force towards the wall at the rear of the garden and cursed loudly.

The disappointment, together with tiredness, icy cold numbness and the atrocious hangover hit me all at once and I started sobbing into my frosty hands.

I accepted that not only was the ticket lost, but also the life-changing moment that may only happen once, had potentially slipped through my fingers. Literally. With two hundred and forty-five million pounds at stake and without giving it a second thought, I'd casually folded a potentially winning ticket into my pocket and through sheer carelessness, lost it.

All my life had been spent dreaming about the moment that things would change; that one day I would find the great wealth that I had so desperately craved. I'd always tried to imagine how I would feel if maybe, just maybe, Lady Luck would shine down on me. And now I was convinced she had, but I had blown it!

I removed my coat and shoes inside the door and I wandered back into the kitchen area to find my mum preparing some lunch.

'Where's Dad?' I asked, sinking into one of the chairs at the breakfast bar, placing my hands onto my hot coffee cup.

Just then Dad wandered into the kitchen. 'I'm here kid. What the hell you doing to my back garden?'

'He's lost his bank card,' Mum said, passing me a sandwich. 'Stick the light on, Bill, would you?'

I was staring up at the ceiling, releasing the slight tension in my neck as the light illuminated. An unbearable, horrific pain smashed me directly between the eyes. I jumped up from the chair holding the back of my head, wincing in pain as the noise levels all around me slowly decreased and my vision blurred.

For the third time this year, a bright light had shone into my eyes, causing excruciating pains inside of my skull. And for the third time this year, I felt my body fall to the floor as I blacked out, thumping the side of my head as I connected with the floor, losing consciousness as I landed.

4

Out cold

The first time I blacked out was just under a year ago, after an all-night party at Tom's house. He'd arranged a get together for our friends to celebrate Erika's birthday and copious amounts of alcohol were consumed by all. That was also the night I almost plucked up the courage to ask Erika out on a date, but as usual and even with a stomach full of booze, I had failed to let her know my true feelings.

I'd woken up early after only an hour or so of snoozing, unable to get back to a state of boozy unconsciousness and stumbled downstairs and outside into the cool morning air. The glaring sunlight contrasted with the dark passageway and it hit me between the eyes as I was instantly consumed with the same, immense pain I'd felt on my way down to my parent's tiled floor.

The pain jabbed at the back of my skull as I tumbled to the ground in the middle of Tom's driveway, blacking out for what I guessed to be only a few seconds. Oddly, the pain was only a short and sharp shooting feeling and lasted a mere moment. I blamed it on too much alcohol.

I never felt the need to share my blackout with anyone and simply dismissed it, continuing with my life as though the event had never taken place.

The second time, five months ago, convinced me that the first episode was not alcohol-related. I was driving home from an afternoon at the shooting range with Tom, perfecting our weaponry skills and picking up where I'd left off in the Marines; an expert marksman. As I approached a set of traffic lights close to my apartment block, a large truck stopped on the opposite side of the road. The guy flashed his main headlights at another vehicle in front and the bright light beamed directly into my eyes. The stabbing pain exploded in the back of my head, only this time it was a longer, more dramatic pain, as though I was taking a heavy blow to the head.

I screamed as the pain gripped my whole body, temporarily paralysing me from head to toe. I'd passed out with the pain and the next thing I remembered was an angry driver behind me, blaring his horn. Sweat was dripping from my face and my heart was racing as I managed to shake off the mini trauma and finish my short journey home. I had no idea how long I'd been 'out.'

Outside my apartment block, I'd sat for at least thirty minutes alone in my car, staring in the rear-view mirror and shaking my head occasionally to see if the pain would return. Strangely, it had disappeared completely. I promised myself a visit to the doctor, but with my hefty work schedule, I'd simply forgotten about it and continued on with my life.

As my skull connected with my parents' hard, tiled floor, my memory bank was sub-consciously replaying the moment I'd purchased the lottery ticket. The trauma I was experiencing, mixed with the intense emotion of possibly losing a winning jackpot ticket, was also affecting me on a subconscious level.

'Mark … Mark … are you okay, son?'

The vision vanished and I was beginning to make out a vague outline of what looked like my dad bent over me, holding my head, obviously trying to figure out what the hell had just happened. I heard sound, but it was a muffled noise like when you stick your fingers in your ear.

I blinked quickly, letting out a long sigh as I stretched out my body, feeling like I had just awoken from a long, deep sleep. My mother, father and two brothers were all leaning over me in complete shock.

As I glanced to my right, I realised I was now in my parents' front room, lying on their large sofa.

'What happened? Did you just faint?' Dad was checking my pulse and temperature.

'I must have,' I replied. 'I haven't eaten today. Maybe it was the reaction from the cold and walking straight into the heat of kitchen. I don't know.'

The pain had once again disappeared from the back of my head.

'Go and get some chocolate out the fridge Andrew, will you? He needs sugar into him now! And Bill, I think we should get you an ambulance.'

My mum was always quick to take charge of a situation.

'It's not Andrew, it's Andy,' he grunted, loathing the fact they continued to use his full name. He disappeared into the kitchen, strolling back with a chocolate bar and tossed it onto my lap. 'For God's sake, he's only fainted. You'd think he died the way you're all going on.'

Although Andy was the bright, articulate member of our family, his distinct lack of compassion was at times, annoying.

'You need to see a doctor, Mark. You don't just faint for no reason.'

I could feel the concern in my mum's voice and tried my best to put her mind at ease. 'Don't worry, we don't need an ambulance. I've had no food today, that's all. The mixture of cold and heat together just hit me.'

Chris, my other brother, brought a towel wrapped around ice cubes and stuck it onto my head.

As they left me to rest on the sofa, my thoughts started to drift again, confused as to what could actually be wrong with me and why, on three separate occasions had a bright light in my eye triggered an immense pain in my head? A visit to the doctor was a must. I would make the call first thing tomorrow morning.

5

An update from Katie Bell

A bar of chocolate and a sugar fuelled cup of British tea actually made me feel better, especially as I was now curled up on the sofa in front of my parents' huge open fire.

Mum had checked on me every ten minutes for the past four hours, eventually giving up when I'd insisted she had nothing to worry about and to just let me sleep for a while. My whole family was now relaxing around the fire as the snow continued to add more inches to the layers outside.

'Mark, have you asked Erika out on a date yet?' Chris, slouched over the end of the sofa we were sharing, grinned sheepishly as he asked the question, obviously aware that if I had asked her and she'd said yes, then the whole of Newcastle would know about it.

'Nope.'

'Well, if you don't ask her soon, then I'm going to try my luck. I've already been with her two best friends and they were a definite let down, so why not go straight for the prize turkey?' He winked at me, then looked directly at the TV before I could retaliate. He wanted a childish reaction from me and generally he would get one, but I kept my cool and simply shrugged off his inconsequence.

A minute passed. 'When I'm rich,' I said, 'she'll only want one member of this household and it certainly won't be you.'

'Oh, here we go,' he laughed, rolling his eyes and sitting up straight. 'You've got issues, Mark. Get in the real world, Peter bloody Pan. Keep dreaming, big brother, and ask out Erika on a date. You've got one week and then I'm going in for the kill.' He stood up and headed towards the door. He ruffled my hair before scarpering into the corridor, leaving the thought annoyingly circling in my head.

'Unofficial reports tell us that an unnamed source, living in Newcastle upon Tyne, has come forward to claim the huge lottery jackpot.' It was that girl Katie Bell again, the pretty reporter I'd seen on the TV in the sports bar. She was back outside Lottery HQ in London. She was continuing to brave the harsh winds and sleet and my eyes almost popped out of their sockets as I tried to register what she'd just said. I cranked up the volume to catch the rest of her report. 'So far, lottery officials are refusing to comment on this new development, but our sources tell us that a few hours ago, a registration attempt was in progress by an unnamed individual. The unprecedented two hundred and forty-five million pounds has been unclaimed for five days now and unconfirmed reports tell us that the claimant was away on business and only realised today that they could be the missing ticket-holder.'

'It's about bloody time. He only had one day left,' Andy said.

My insides were churning and my mouth had begun to salivate profusely. I stood up and casually left the room before dashing to the downstairs toilet, yanking open the door and locking it behind me. I stood over the toilet taking deep breaths and trying hard to resist the urge, but it was no use. I emptied the entire contents from my stomach into the bowl.

I'd wasted my time pulling my flat apart, my clothes, the local store and my parent's garden, not to mention every pathway on route. My frantic searching and my emotional rollercoaster had all been for nothing. Why the hell was I surprised, though?

'I don't believe it,' I grunted, grabbing a paper towel to wipe my face. Once again, I was staring at my reflection, dabbing my mouth with a towel, and taking a few long breaths to calm myself down.

I flushed the toilet, replaced the towel and headed back to the living room. I decided it was time I was on my way. I needed to walk and clear my head. 'I'm off home,' I said, grabbing my coat on the way back to the living room.

'Why don't you just stay the night?' Mum said.

'I'm fine Mum. I've got loads to do and my flat's upside down. The snow's not too bad just now, so it's probably best I get off before it starts again.'

'Promise you will call when you get home then, do you hear me?' she replied, pulling up the collar on my coat and kissing me on the cheek.

'Course.'

I left the warm house and crunched into the snow down the pathway, making my way out of their street. I aimlessly walked to nowhere in particular. The last place I wanted to go was back to my flat, so flipped open my mobile phone and called Tom.

'Alright Tom,' I said as he answered.

'Alright Dreamer?' he replied.

'What you up to?'

'Well, at this precise moment' he replied pausing, 'I am kicking my computers arse on World Cup soccer.'

'I need a drink,' I replied.

'My bar is always open lad, how long you gonna be?'

'Ten minutes,' I replied, flipping the phone closed as I picked up my pace.

6

Erika

Tom lived in an enormous house set back on its own grounds around a private, gated estate with 24-hour security. His father, who owned specialist motor dealerships all over the region, sold high-class supercars to clients with colossal bank accounts. Tom worked for his father at home and at various dealerships around the area, getting paid a hefty wage for his efforts. I never, ever found out his exact role or job title.

His gorgeous sister Erika had recently finished her law degree and was now following my lead by taking a few months off to relax and decide her next move.

I approached the giant black gates to the estate, pushed the buzzer on the side of the post, and waited.

'Who is it?'

'Hi, it's … it's Mark.' I recognised Erika's voice.

'Oh, hi Mark, won't you come in?'

The towering gates creaked and groaned into life as they sluggishly inched open. The picturesque driveway lay untouched, covered in virgin snow. I struggled to follow the long, winding road uphill towards the luxury six-bedroom house. High, thin trees lined the pathway and, with the fallen snow resting on the bare branches, gave rather a festive and quite picturesque scene to my climb to reach the front door.

The enormous house had been restored and converted from a historic building and was somewhat overwhelming from this distance. The mature oak front door was a magnificent centrepiece. Concrete pillars held up the large porch entrance, which was decorated beautifully with an oversized white Christmas tree that twinkled with bright, festive lights.

To the left was a large extension that had been recently added, housing an indoor swimming pool and gymnasium over two floors. If only … I was back into daydreaming mode.

To the right of the main area of the property was Tom's father's 'off limits' garage, where only invitees could view his expensive, collector edition motorcars. His latest acquisition was the Maserati 3500 GT Touring, Series One - 1960. At a cool one hundred and fifty-five thousand Pounds, it was his new pride and joy, and I was convinced he loved his cars more than his wife. Although I would never say that out loud.

Erika was waiting by the white decorated tree to my sheer joy. Beautiful as always, elegant and sexy as hell. She instantly warmed my insides as I approached the large porch area.

My heart began to race as I took in her beauty; her short blonde hair, parted just off centre, was pleasantly in line with her piercingly light green eyes. Her complexion was clean, her skin smooth. No make-up was needed to radiate her beauty. Dressed in a light, cream dress which flowed down to her knees, hugging her figure perfectly, she oozed charisma in the simplest of ways. Her bright pink slippers, which were shaped as Father Christmas, although amusing, merely added to her sex appeal. She made the long, cold trek worth every step.

'Hey Mark,' she called out, smiling and brushing her hair back from her eyes as she glanced to the floor, 'Tom's upstairs, do come on in.'

'Thanks.' My voice sounded gruff. I followed her into the house, along the corridor and up the large, winding staircase. I'm convinced she has always been aware of my feelings and likes to tease me

33

slightly in her own way. If only I had the confidence to take things further. If only I actually grew some balls.

I watched her as we climbed the stairs; her pert butt cheeks wiggling seductively with each step. She left me at Tom's door and gave me a grin as she strolled down to her room at the end of the long corridor. What I wouldn't give to follow her into her bedroom and tell her how I feel. Maybe engage in a few other things too.

Back to reality, as she waved at me and closed her door. I forcefully bashed on Tom's door and walked in, finding him completely engrossed in his computer console. I walked over to the bar area of his ridiculously large bedroom and poured myself a large vodka and Diet Coke.

The room, which was at least five times the size of my flat, had everything you could possibly need to survive your whole life without ever leaving it. A mammoth ninety-inch wide-screen TV was fixed to the wall in the centre of the room, hooked up to the latest computer consoles as well as cable TV. Two large leather chairs in the middle of the room were his 'console and cinema experience' and would only be used when he was involved in a game or a decent movie. With in-built speakers in the headrest, massage functions, a pint-sized cup holder and recliner function, the chairs were the ultimate boy's luxury.

On the opposite side of his room, where I was standing, was a full-size bar filled with beer, wines, and spirits. There was also a small office area, with a desk that was valued at the same price as a small family car, and his proudly named 'playpen', which consisted of a dartboard, three of the latest arcade machines, four separate, but equally expensive console machines, and a wall unit full of at least a thousand games. A second ninety-inch 3D-TV set was fixed to the wall.

Finally, the latest in Formula One technology. My absolute favourite toy was the F1 racing car simulator, fully updated with that year's Grand Prix locations from around the world.

Tom's father, who was more connected than the queen, had been reliably informed that one of the Formula One teams was purchasing a new and improved simulator and would only sell the machine to a trusted, non-competing party, A few weeks later, the item was quietly sold to him for an undisclosed fee.

'Hey Dreamer, didn't hear you come in,' Tom said, glancing up at me and then straight back to his game.

'Yeah, your sister let me in.'

'What's up with you, then? I can't believe you are drinking after what we put over our necks yesterday.'

'It's Christmas,' I lied.

I couldn't muster the courage to tell him I'd spent the whole day searching for a lottery ticket. Apart from feeling physically sick, I was utterly embarrassed at my ridiculous shenanigans.

'Go on then, pour me one and I'll join you. Can't have you drinking on your own now can we?'

As I strolled back to his bar and found a glass, I filled it generously with two shots of vodka. Tom flicked his console off and I passed him his drink. I flopped into his large leather chair. I tried to block out my disappointment and stupidity, sitting quietly with my own thoughts as the chair automatically began to massage my back.

7

4,8,16,19,27,44, 2 and 9

Three large glasses of vodka later, the alcohol was now alive in my bloodstream and I was feeling slightly more relaxed than a few hours earlier. 'Another?' I asked and got up. I staggered towards the bar.

'Why not?' Tom replied, his cheeks glowing along with mine at the presence of vodka rushing around his veins. He flicked over the channel as I poured the large measures into the glasses and watched the beginning of yet another news report. BREAKING NEWS, the ticker tape across the bottom of the screen. I ceased pouring and asked him to turn up the volume.

It was a local reporter. 'With the rumours in full flow that a lucky person had claimed to be the winner of the World Lottery Jackpot, we can now confirm that his claim was, in fact, untrue. Lottery HQ has officially declared that no such ticket and no such person has put claim to the enormous jackpot prize. I repeat, the jackpot remains unclaimed.'

As I watched, slightly shellshocked, a huge crowd of people had gathered around the store and the reporter, as he stood with a large umbrella to shield himself from the snow. 'I am here at Bill's News, the newsagent store in a suburb of Newcastle upon Tyne, where the two hundred and forty-five million pound winning lottery ticket was purchased. Bill, the owner, joins me now.' He turned to Bill. 'Tell me, sir, how have things been at your store since the world was made aware that you sold the largest jackpot ticket in history?'

Bill looked a little stunned, clearly uncomfortable to be thrust into the limelight. 'It's been pretty crazy, I guess,' he said in a monotone voice. 'I've never seen so many people in my shop. I cannot believe that the winner hasn't yet come forward.'

The knot had returned to my stomach as the realisation of what I was watching began to sink in again. Either the person claiming to be the winner was a hoax, or the media had invented the ticket winner to enhance their story. The chances and possibilities of my ticket being the actual winner had slammed itself back into play.

'Can you believe this shit?' Tom asked, sitting up in his chair.

'Unbelievable,' I replied.

'Why the hell would you buy a ticket and then wait this long to claim it? The prick probably hasn't even checked it.' He turned to me. 'What would you do with two hundred and forty-five million Pounds, mate?'

I couldn't even give him an answer. The news report had me stunned into silence.

'Oh, the fun you could have,' said Tom, leaning back in his chair. 'I think I would travel abroad and have sex with as many foreign women as physically possible. I'd travel on private jets and stay in five-star hotels.'

I held onto my emotions and kept my lips tightly shut.

'I'm starving,' said Tom, changing the subject as he hopped up from his chair and walked over to his office desk.

'Me too.'

He returned with a few takeaway menus. He threw them onto my lap.

'What do you fancy, then? Indian, Chinese …'

'Nah.'

'What about a pizza?'

And there it was, the moment of realisation as though God had cast an invisible bolt of lightning into the room and the electricity had somehow reset my brain. And things were crystal clear, a concise action replay of exactly what had happened. 'Tom, I have to run. I think I left the gas on in my house.'

'But mate, you said you were starving.'

I launched myself from the chair and without another word ran out of his room. I heard him call after me as my heart, which had taken a huge battering over the last few days, began to bulge out of my chest. I sprinted down the large staircase, taking three steps at a time, and barged through the heavy oak door into the freezing cold air.

Clambering down the driveway, I pushed through the deep snow towards the automatic gates. At the bottom of the drive, I triggered the automatic infrared sensor as the gates creaked slowly open. With a gap just big enough to get my body through, I forced myself out into the street, turned left, and began to pick up the pace, trying not to slip on the icy pathway. My mind skipped into overdrive and I became completely unaware of the roads, forgetting to look for cars that may have been driving through the slippery tracks. I needed to get home as quickly as I could.

I ran as fast as my legs could carry me, completely immune to the cold sweat already freezing my face. My mind and my physical being were currently two separate entities, and there was room for only one emotion right now.

My fitness levels had significantly decreased over the past few weeks, but at this moment in time, I would have beat Usain Bolt back to my apartment block.

I approached the towering site of the Tyne Bridge, only a few minutes from my flat as I galloped through the thick snow like Shergar. My heartbeat was at least three times its normal speed and the knot tightened inside of me as a stitch started to develop. My body cried stop, but there was no time to lose, no time to slow down and catch my breath.

My apartment block came into view and I crossed the last street and slid around the corner. I burst through the door and by-passing the lift, dashed up the stairs two at a time. I was now completely out of breath and ready to collapse onto the floor into a heap, so I bent over the handrail to give myself a moment to get my breath back. Eventually, I reached level four and approached my front door, pulled out the key, and let myself in.

The sweat was dripping down my face as I approached the kitchen and sprinted towards the large unit at the end of the bench. I grabbed the top drawer handle and held it in my right hand. I took a long, deep breath and opened it.

I pulled out the half dozen takeaway food menus that lay inside the drawer and located the exact same menu that Tom had thrown at me ten or fifteen minutes earlier. 'Pedro's Pizzas. The Best Pizza's in Town.' The menu that had triggered a drunken memory.

'Oh shit, oh shit.' I flicked the remaining menus to the floor, holding the 'Pedro Pizza' menu tightly in my hand. I recalled how I had arrived home in my drunken state, staggered into the kitchen, and grabbed the menu. I'd ordered a large meat feast and pigged out in front of the TV.

For some reason I thought it would be a great idea to keep everything inside one of the pizza menus for safekeeping. Unfortunately, the memory of this event had completely escaped me until Tom had thrown the Pedro's menu onto my lap.

I stared blankly at the front cover for what seemed like an eternity, praying that the ticket would be inside.

After two hard, deep breaths, I dragged a finger across the front page, holding it there for a second, chanting a prayer to a God I didn't believe in. I was teetering on the edge as the life-changing moment lay right in front of me. I grabbed the spine of the menu, tipped the menu upside down and gave it a little shake. I closed my eyes and distinctly heard something hit the floor.

I opened my eyes and gazed down. A handful of ten and twenty-pound notes were lying on the tiled floor. I picked up the pile of money and fanned it out. My heart stopped dead. There it was, between two notes: a folded up red lottery ticket.

I reached for it and held it in my right hand as the rest of the notes felt to the floor. I dropped to my knees and burst into tears. The emotional journey I'd experienced over the last few days had all come down to this single moment.

The ticket may not even be a winner, but fate had assured me of at least a chance.

I sobbed tears of joy and elation and let my emotions flow as my tears turned to laughter. There was only one thing left to do as I returned to the lounge and reached for the newspaper, still open at the results page.

One by one, I checked the numbers of the results and then the numbers of the lucky dip line on my ticket. My hands were shaking as I checked, double-checked and triple-checked the numbers.

4, I have 4.

8, I have 8.

16, I have 16

19, I have 19

27, I have 27

44, I have 44

World Number 2, I have world number 2

World number 9, I have world number 9.

Realisation sank in.

I'd just won 245 million Pounds.

8

Realisation sets in

One cannot describe the feeling you experience when you not only know you've won a large jackpot, but the amount of money concerned is more than you could actually comprehend. Almost a quarter of a billion British pounds were waiting to be claimed and could change not only my life, but everyone else's around me.

I sat back on my sofa, dazed and in a cold sweat, still trying to come to terms with this surreal turn of events. At least fifty times, I checked and re-checked the ticket. I was, without question, in possession of the winning ticket.

No matter how many times you sit and think of how you would feel if one day it was your turn, the sheer elation is one of indescribable joy and one with unthinkable possibilities.

I need never work again, never want for anything in my entire existence. I could live the rest of my life without even touching my bank balance and still live like a king. Those sentences alone were beyond the comprehension of where I had come from in life.

After checking and rechecking the numbers, I had screamed so hard and loud in a joyful song that my throat was actually hurting. My flat was literally flipped upside down when I ran into every room and jumped all over my bed, sofa and tables, shouting with happiness.

As I sat, now panting and sweating in my living room, I tried to get a grip on myself and think about what the hell I would do next. The press were sitting poised, ready to attack the moment they unearthed who had scooped the world's biggest lottery jackpot, and that was something I did not want to share with the world. It would undoubtedly destroy any privacy my family and friends had ever enjoyed, not to mention the huge vulnerability and security risk.

Like my mum had said, she didn't even know if she would want the burden of that sort of money surrounding her.

I could not, and would not, subject my family to a life of hiding or media invasion and had already made the decision that I would do my utmost to keep my identity private. I would tell my family and friends in my own time and not make any rash decisions that could prove costly further down the line. My brothers were still very young and immature, so handing over several million and asking them to be quiet would be impossible.

The back of the ticket explained in detail what you had to do to claim, and as I only had a few hours left, I needed to get dialling pretty quickly.

My hands were still shaking uncontrollably; my life was about to change, to be turned upside down in the next sixty seconds and as I picked up my phone, I inhaled a few long, deep breaths and prepared myself for all of my dreams to hurtle into fruition.

I dialled the number.

'Good afternoon, Lottery prize line, this is Melinda. How can I help you?'

My mouth was dry. I couldn't manage a single word.

'My name is Melinda. Are you calling to claim a prize?'

At last the words came out of my mouth. 'Yes … I … I have a winning jackpot ticket … I think. I'm sorry, I'm shaking like a leaf.'

'Take your time, sir. Can I ask your name?'

'It's Mark. Mark Davidson'

'Okay, Mark, it's nice to talk to you. Now, can you tell me which jackpot ticket you believe you have won?'

'Yes … I, I'm not really prepared for this, but I believe I have the winning ticket from the World Lottery.'

'Okay, Mark, if you have the ticket then, firstly, may I congratulate you? Would you please confirm the winning numbers on your ticket for me?'

'Yes. They are, 04, 16, 19, 27, 28 and 44 and I also have the two lucky numbers 02 and 09.' I read each number precisely and slowly.

'Well, Mark,' she replied. 'Those are indeed the correct winning numbers. At the bottom, there is a unique barcode and a serial number with a mixture of twenty-three numbers and letters. If you could read those to me, please.'

It took me almost a minute to read the lengthy number as I paused after each, giving Melinda plenty of time to write it down and then repeat it back to me. After a brief silence, she asked me to repeat the serial number for a second time slowly. I heard her whisper something to a colleague under her breath.

I repeated the serial number and Melinda seemed to burst into life.

'Congratulations Mark, if you indeed have the ticket in hand, I can confirm this serial number matches our records as a winning jackpot ticket! Okay, the first thing you need to do is write down your name and address clearly on the ticket. If you turn the ticket over, there is a small area for you to do that. Please do this while you are on the phone, as this is very important for security reasons.'

'I've already done that,' I managed to say softly, wiping the sweat from my brow.

'Excellent, Mark. Now if you can tell me your address and postcode, we will send a driver to you immediately. He will take you to your nearest Regional Lottery office. Time is of the essence. We have less than three hours to get you to the lottery offices and input your ticket into the regional machine. Please make sure you bring the ticket and some photographic identification. Also,' she continued, 'please pack a bag for a few nights away from home. We suggest you stay away from your own house for a few days, while we complete the transaction and talk you through the procedures. We will go into more detail once you arrive at the regional offices.'

I gave her my address.

'Okay, your driver is on his way. If you give me your mobile phone number he will call you once he arrives.'

'No problem,' I said and sat on the sofa, letting out a huge sigh.

'The driver's name is Sidney Thompson. He will be driving a Black BMW, registration NC1 LTY. His contact number is 0700 13322.'

I wrote down the driver's details.

'That's all, Mark, the driver will be with you soon.'

The biggest phone call of my life ended, and for five minutes or more I sat and stared into space. Slightly dazed, I stood up and walked to the bedroom, filled an overnight bag with enough clothes for a few days and walked around the flat, unplugging every piece of electrical equipment.

I got into the shower and washed faster than I had ever done in my life, changed, picked up my house keys, wallet and mobile phone, and put on my coat. As I zipped up my coat and walked to the front door, my phone rang.

'Good afternoon, is this Mr Mark Davidson?'

'That's me,' I replied.

'This is Sidney Thompson. I'm a driver for the UK National Lottery Service. I am outside your house now. I believe you are expecting me?'

'Yes, I am. Give me two minutes.' I put the lottery ticket in my wallet and locked the door with the phone still to my ear.

I bound down the apartment steps and out into the cold air. My heart continued to pound rapidly as I approached the black car. Sidney turned to see me approaching and I gave him a wave.

'Mr Davidson, I presume,' he replied as he opened the driver's door and stepped out. 'Very pleased to meet you. I'm Sidney.'

'Pleased to meet you too,' I said, shaking his hand.

He opened the rear door of the black BMW, took my bag, and put it in the boot. I climbed in and watched him as he returned to the driver's seat. He was dressed immaculately in a jet black, shiny suit, crisp white shirt and black tie. Well over six feet tall and just as wide. He had a strange, mixed accent; southern English but with a hint of German, but I couldn't be sure.

The car was magnificent and had the distinct smell you find in a brand-new car. The seats were soft grey leather and as I sat back, I could feel the heated seats warming my cold backside.

The driver and front passenger headrests were fitted with small TV screens and a telephone handset was installed into the centre compartment of the rear seats. The windows were tinted black. As Sidney started the engine, it purred quietly into life and inched forward away from the apartment block.

We drove cautiously out of the city through the thick layers of snow whilst Sidney confirmed he would drive me to the regional office, where I would be met by the regional manager. Later, when the formalities were complete, he would take me to a hotel.

I sat in silence for the rest of the journey, nervous as hell but excited at the prospect of the next few hours.

The regional offices were fairly small, maybe big enough for twenty people or so. There were five other cars in the parking spaces and as I glanced towards the main building, I could see a few people excitedly milling around the reception area.

As I exited the car, a well-dressed gentleman stepped forward and shook my hand. 'Mr Davidson, Brian Holding. I'm the Northeast regional manager for the lottery service, and may I say it's a pleasure to meet you. Congratulations, congratulations.' He smiled at me for what seemed like an eternity. He glanced over my shoulder towards the car. 'Nobody with you, no family members?'

'No, I thought it best to keep this as low-key as possible. We are a very private family and I wish to do my best to try and keep it that way.'

'Of course, Mr Davidson, we completely understand.'

He gestured me towards the building. 'Please follow me and we can get things moving for you.'

We walked through two office doors into a large reception area where two female assistants were waiting anxiously, holding clipboards and grinning from ear to ear.

He guided me over to a machine. 'We scan all the winning tickets into the machine and this will confirm your ticket as valid. Once that's done you can breathe a sigh of relief. Do you have the ticket?'

I noticed his hand slightly shaking as I handed him the ticket, but it was nothing compared to my nervous rattle. 'Don't lose it will you,' I joked, trying to smile through gritted teeth. My stomach was churning and I twitched nervously as he held my ticket, my eyes never leaving it as we stood by the machine.

The two assistants were with us, clipboards at the ready, and Brian inserted the ticket into the machine. I can safely say that this was the most frightened I had ever been in my entire life and I held my breath as the ticket was slowly inserted into the machine.

For what seemed like an eternity, the machine made no sound and for a few anxious seconds, my heart almost stopped as I willed it to do something. And then … it happened. The machine printed a small ticket. Brian took and scanned it over a glass panel. It let out two loud, high-pitched beeps.

'Congratulations, Mark,' he said, 'you have just won two hundred and forty-five million, eight hundred and nine thousand, seven hundred and seventy-five Pounds.'

The words circled my head for a second or two as I started to shake uncontrollably, feeling the blood rush from my head. I held up my finger, asking for a moment as my mouth filled with saliva and I became weak at the knees. The two girls moved in close. They felt sure I was about to drop to the floor but I found the strength in my legs, rushed back through the reception doors into the car park and vomited the contents of my stomach into a flowerbed.

9

Dutch Courage

I took a few deep breaths as one assistant approached me outside with a bottle of water. 'Are you okay?'

'I'm fine, yeah, thanks. I think everything kind of just hit me, you know?'

'You're not the first and won't be the last,' she replied, passing me a few tissues.

Walking back into the office, I thanked the assistant and apologised to everyone for my mini trauma.

With a little chuckle, Brian placed his hand on my shoulder. 'Mark, please don't apologise. This is a huge shock for you and will take some time to get used to. Tell me and forgive me for prying, but are you sure you don't want any of your family with you?'

'It's okay,' I replied, hesitating. 'I've thought about this for a long time and no, I couldn't drop this on them at the moment. I need to take stock, tell them when the time is right … in my own time, maybe when the whole media frenzy thing calms down.'

'I fully understand. The press is asking questions on an hourly basis and you are well within your rights to have complete confidentiality.'

I was taken to another room. They confirmed that the money would be transferred into a new bank account that was now activated. The account would be a medium interest savings account. I would be earning a modest two hundred and thirty-five thousand pounds per week in interest payments alone. My jaw almost hit the floor, realising that was almost a million every month. I was about to be paid the equivalent of any sports or movie star for sitting at home with my feet up. It hardly seemed fair, but I would take it, nonetheless.

After sifting through the finer details, I was introduced to my appointed bank manager, who gave me all of my private account details, ready for the funds to be transferred. He advised me to have an accountant to look after my affairs and recommended one from the bank who usually dealt with lottery winners. It would take forty-eight hours for the funds to be transferred, so he handed me a temporary 'charge card'. He explained that for the next two days, a temporary account with access to one million pounds was now active and asked me to sign the card, which already had my name inscribed into it.

Any money I spent would be deducted from the initial transfer on the day of completion. The seventy thousand pounds in interest which would accumulate in the next two days would also be added to the final transfer amount.

After the bank meeting, I was visited by a psychiatrist. This was part of the routine for any new multi-millionaires as this could be a traumatic time for the ill prepared. He was in his late fifties, an American and brimming with the usual over the top, chirpy confidence. He sat with me for another hour, explaining that he'd experienced many cases in which people had won huge sums of money and been unable to cope with their sudden, newly found wealth. 'Some people will simply spend like there is no tomorrow and watch their vast wealth diminish, often becoming addicted to spending or gambling and unable to control themselves. Some have given all of their money to family, charities, homeless people and beggars on the street and before they know it, have little left to make a life for themselves.'

He urged me to take some time and analyse everything before parting with a penny and said that if I needed to talk, then he was always available. For a fee, of course.

After hours of de-briefing, talking and completing various documents, we were almost done. My friendly regional manager was the last person to see me. 'Okay, Mark, I believe everything is in order at our end. Many congratulations, I really hope you enjoy this with your family and friends and that you listen and act on all the advice that was offered today.' He passed me a business card. 'Any questions?'

'Thanks for all of your help, Brian,' I replied. 'Just one more thing. I really need to keep this private and whatever happens, I need to keep myself out of the public eye. I need time to think and decide what to do next. I don't want the added pressures of the media, that will only lead to our lives being ruined and our privacy vanishing forever.'

I was concerned about everyone finding out my identity, but Brian assured me that the privacy agreement we had both signed only moments ago guaranteed that the media would not be told who I was.

I left the offices with a briefcase full of documents and Sidney drove me to the hotel. At their expense, I was booked in for three nights at Newcastle's only 5-star hotel, La Maison, on the quayside, allowing me time away from home to reflect.

Checking into the hotel, I found that I was booked into the largest suite the hotel had. It stood over two floors at the very top of the hotel and was complete with butler service, spa, cinema room, and my own private gymnasium.

I let out a shout when the butler left. I screamed in elation at the top of my voice like an excited child and ran around the room. I felt like stripping naked and sprinting through the hotel.

My dream had come true and I was now free to do whatever I wanted, whenever I wanted. The euphoria was like nothing I had ever experienced, and I bounced up and down on what looked like a ridiculously expensive sofa.

My temporary insanity eventually faded, and I stopped screaming, settling onto the chair at the rear of the living room. I laughed to myself. I laughed hard and as tears of joy rolled down my cheeks, I could still not quite believe what had just happened to me. This time tomorrow, I would have earned over thirty-five thousand pounds in interest on my new winnings. That was more than I would have earned in a full year.

'Good afternoon Mr Davidson, how can I help you?' the butler said when I dialled zero on the handset.

'Would you be able to send me a bottle of champagne please, number seventy-six on the menu? Oh and some strawberries, please, and chilled water.'

'Of course, sir, would there be anything else?'

'No thanks, not just now.'

Within moments, a bottle of Cristal Special Edition, chilled to an icy temperature, a large silver tray of strawberries and a huge jug of iced water, arrived at my room.

I checked the price of the champagne. At four thousand, five hundred pounds per bottle, I felt slightly guilty, remembering everything that had been told to me regarding lavish spending, but I figured if I spent less than thirty-five thousand pounds in a day then I had still made a profit.

'I'm quite good at this accounting thing,' I said to myself as I popped the cork of the bottle, sending it flying to the other side of the room. I poured myself a glass and ambled over to the enormous window overlooking the city. The view was breath-taking. The sun setting in the distance shimmered off the snow-covered streets and as I sipped on the expensive bubbles, I could not have been happier.

I had always loved my own company, spending time in my own space, which definitely spanned from my youth. I had enjoyed reflecting on life. Always the dreamer.

My mind drifted to my family, my friends, the people I cared about. How and what would I tell them if I wanted to keep a low profile? How would they take it? Would my friends turn greedy and demand money from me? Would my family be forced into hiding because of the reporters?

I needed time for things to sink in but tonight would be my night, my time to celebrate. Everyone had always told me to stop dreaming and get into the real world. But tonight the real world belonged to me.

I finished my first glass of cold champagne and poured myself a second. I looked up at the mirror. My face radiated a slightly red glow as the alcohol started to take effect, easing the tension I'd been feeling all day.

I dialled zero on the handset again and ordered a plate of sandwiches and snacks as I flicked on the TV. Better off getting something in my stomach, as twice today I had emptied its contents. I decided to stay clear of the news channels and opted for one of the twenty-four-hour, non-stop music channels instead.

The butler dropped off my snacks and as I sat with my thoughts, I began to feel a little guilty as a love song played out on the screen. Although I enjoyed my own company, I would have loved nothing better than to call my family, or even my best mate Tom, and tell them what had just happened to me.

But not yet.

I grabbed my mobile phone and scanned my contacts list. With two glasses of champagne firmly settling into my system, I was filled with thoughts of the one person I would really have loved to be with me right now.

I scrolled straight down to Erika's name and stared at her number. She had always teased me every time we met and I'm convinced that she maybe had a soft spot for me, but still, I'd never found the courage to just ask her out on a date. Surely now things were different and I could offer her something that not many others could. Surely now I was a multi-millionaire, I could take my chance?

I couldn't tell her about what had happened, not yet anyway. How would I ever know that she would date me for me and not the money? Was I bold enough to simply ask her out for dinner? I'd been threatening to do it for such a long time, so why not today?

I sat back and closed my eyes, reminding myself of her beauty. Her silky blonde hair, those piercing green eyes, and that gorgeous face. She was a vision of beauty. Why had I left it so long to find the courage to even let her know how I felt? Her smile melted my heart every time she looked at me, and yet I'd never found the courage to just let her know.

I opened my eyes and walked over to the half-empty bottle of champagne and re-filled my glass. The alcohol was starting to settle nicely inside, and I was starting to find a little courage.

What did I have to lose? Grow some balls, will you? Call her, she can only say no.

I stared at the phone, willing myself to dial the number. I turned down the volume of the TV, my finger hovered over the green dial button of the phone.

'Just do it will you,' I shouted, as I pushed the button. The nervous, knotted feeling in my stomach returned, far worse than earlier on. I drained the rest of the glass as the plan formulated in my head. How could she possibly refuse? I put the phone to my ear. I took a deep breath and exhaled as my heart pounded with excitement.

A sweet voice, calm and serene, answered the phone with a simple, 'Hello Mark.'

The beat of my heart doubled its pace.

'Hi … er … how are you?' My voice was shaky, nervous, and I'm sure it actually squeaked.

'Fine, thanks for asking.'

'Well, Erika … I … er … well, I wondered if you would, that is you don't have to, but I wondered if you would like to have dinner with me sometime, maybe, I mean only if you want.' My sentence made partial sense, I think, and I prayed to God I did not have to repeat it.

'You want to take me on a date, you mean, Mark?' she replied, giggling.

'Er … yes, a date, a dinner date if that's okay?'

'Of course I'd love to. Why has it taken you this long to ask me?'

I almost choked and took a large gulp of air before continuing. 'If I can be blunt, you're beautiful and I thought maybe you were out of my league if I'm honest, but …'

I took another sip of champagne.

'You've made me blush, Mark. Of course, you can take me to dinner, and don't be silly, I am way in your league.' Her voice was soft and gentle.

'Is tonight too soon?'

'Tonight?'

'Yes, I know, it's short notice, but the thing is I could only get a table at La Maison for tonight. They're booked up solid for the next month.'

My plan worked a treat. I could hear the surprise in her voice.

'La Maison!'

'Yes.'

'But that place will cost a fortune.'

'I know, but you're worth it and I figured our first date should be a little out of the ordinary.'

'I don't know what to say, but you need to give me a few hours to get ready.'

'Okay. Will 7.30 be good?'

'Yes, absolutely. Shall we get a taxi together? I can call one if you like.'

Thinking on my feet I said, 'I … er … I'll sort it, no problem, I'll see you then.'

'Okay great, see you.'

And with that, she was gone.

The smile on my face was even bigger than my smile that morning when it was confirmed that I was a quarter billionaire.

10

MI6

'Sir, it's happened.'

'It's about time. Do we have our people in place? Who is it?'

'Yes, sir. Some young lad in his twenties supposedly lost his ticket but found it at the last minute, we are running background checks now. He's at the La Maison Hotel and we've set the wheels in motion.'

'Okay. The money will be transferred fully in three days to the new account set up for him. Keep the team on the ground and stick to him like glue. Speak to Agent Gray and tell her she has a green light. Tap his phone and tag him. I want to know everything. I want to know if he takes a fucking piss and how long it takes him. You know what to do, find out everything about him. No stone unturned. Keep me updated. I may leave Moscow earlier than planned.'

'Of course, sir.'

'This is a big one. There is no doubt the Tycoon will pull every resource available to him, so this will make them vulnerable. Let's nail this son of a bitch and his whole fucking troop.'

The phone went dead.

11

A Dinner Date

I refilled my glass with the last drops of bubbly as a mild panic set in.

I called my friendly butler, explaining that I'd travelled extremely light and could he recommend a store where I'd be able to purchase a suit, shirt and shoes at short notice.

'Of course sir,' he said, 'The hotel has a Gucci and an Armani Store which are open for the next few hours, they will be happy to assist you. They are on the ground floor next to the dining room. Just add anything to the room account and you can settle it on your departure.'

Gucci and Armani! I was thinking more Marks and Spencer because it had briefly escaped me how much I was worth. Well, why the hell not Gucci and Armani? I grabbed my room key and headed down to the first floor.

It was like an Aladdin's bloody cave down there. I selected the Armani store first, as they had suits and shirts on display that looked more to my taste. As I entered the store the salesman, dressed smartly in a dark blue suit and freshly polished shoes, came towards me, obviously sensing a sale.

'Mr Davidson, I believe?' he asked, holding out his hand.

'Yes,' I replied, obliging the handshake.

'Your butler forewarned me you were on your way. My name is Carl, pleased to meet you. Now, what are we looking for?'

'I need a new shirt, new suit, some underwear, socks, belt and some new shoes.'

The look on his face told me I was about to make this guy a month's worth of commission in about thirty minutes.

'Not a problem, sir. We have the finest clothing money can buy.'

Within a record twenty minutes, Carl had helped me select all the items I needed for my dinner date, including a ludicrously expensive bottle of aftershave. What the hell, I bought an extra suit, two extra pairs of shoes and a new wallet.

At a total of just over four thousand Pounds, this was easily the most expensive shopping trip I'd ever experienced, and I must admit, I loved every minute of it. Selecting items that you really desire without even glancing at the price tag, would seriously take some getting used too.

Bidding farewell to Carl and leaving a rather generous tip, I stopped by my butler's office. I had an idea and he had been so helpful thus far, he was sure to be able to assist.

Bob, my butler, and I made small talk. He was semi-retired and was at the hotel temporarily as the usual full-time butler was at home, sick. It was clear he was way past retirement age, but he told me he needed to earn some extra income. His wife was in a wheelchair and needed to be cared for round the clock.

He got to work on my first request immediately, arranging the hotel's Mercedes saloon to be available for us. A driver would collect me at 7:10 p.m. at reception and then drive me to Erika's house, where we would collect her and drive back to the hotel's restaurant.

Bob booked us a romantic private booth for dinner at the hotel's three Michelin star restaurant. I hadn't been lying to Erika. It had one of the largest waiting lists for dining in the country. He also arranged for the local florist to decorate the table, a dozen white roses and a bottle of Cristal on ice. He promised everything would be perfect. 'Leave it to me, sir,' he said.

I floated on air back to my room, happier than I could ever remember, making a mental note to leave something for Bob after my three days in the hotel.

It had taken me nearly an hour to get myself showered and shaved. I had more champagne as I dressed. I'd opted for a black suit with black shirt and slim black tie. My shiny new shoes gave the twinkle that you only get with a brand-new pair and I'd even purchased new, black Armani socks for the occasion. I felt like a million bucks and I wanted everything to be absolutely perfect.

I gazed into the full-length mirror and lost myself in the moment. I was of average height and, with my army training and gym regime, had maintained a fairly muscular frame. A frame that now looked rather good in this well-cut suit. It's quite amazing how good you feel in an expensive suit. Such a contrast to my youth, where at times I would detest the reflection.

The telephone rang and I quickly snapped out of my daydream.

'Mr Davidson, your car is ready, sir,' Bob said.

'Thanks, be down in two.'

One last glance in the mirror, a few more squirts of my new aftershave, and I was ready. I headed down to meet Bob, who smiled as I walked into reception.

'Looking great, sir,' he said, shaking my hand. 'The car is outside, please follow me.'

As we walked out of the hotel, a shiny black Merc was parked up, with the driver perched at the door. The car was practically brand new; sexy, stylish and glistening in the cool moonlight. The temperature had dipped to minus six, but for the first time in weeks, it had actually stopped snowing.

'Enjoy tonight, sir. Everything has been arranged as requested,' Bob said, ushering me towards the car.

'Thanks, Bob. I can't thank you enough.'

The driver opened my door as I approached and gave a slight bow, tapping the peak of his hat.

I stepped inside and sat on the amazingly comfortable and generously heated, soft-leather seats. As he closed the door, for a split second, alone inside this beautiful machine, I actually felt like somebody.

'Good evening, Mr Davidson, my name is Gregor,' he said. 'We should get to our destination in twenty minutes if no delays.' His accent was broken German or Russian; I couldn't tell which. Why are all limo drivers foreign?

'Okay, great,' I said, smiling at him through his rear-view mirror. Not for the first time that evening, I was feeling anxious; my palms starting to perspire with the heat from the seat. My heart rate had once again increased.

This was a big deal to me, my first date with Erika.

I was doing so well back at the hotel in my room. My confidence was high and I felt on top of the world. But this was now a reality; I felt like a kid on his first day of school. 'What if she didn't like me that way? What if I failed to make conversation or bored her to tears?

The questions came at me thick and fast and the more I thought about them, the more I panicked. I dropped the electric window slightly and allowed some cold air to filter into the car.

'Get a grip on yourself,' I whispered. 'You can do this. Treat her like a lady and you will be fine. It's not as if she's a bloody stranger!' I took more deep breaths, then concentrated on regulating my breathing and before I could get any more nauseous, we approached the security gates of Erika's house. Gregor got out of the car and pressed the buzzer on the side of the post. I recognised Tom's voice who gave a simple 'Yup' as a reply.

'Good evening, sir. I am the driver for Meester Davidson. We are here to collect Miss Erika.'

Tom burst out laughing. 'It's a joke. Mr Davidson doesn't have a bloody driver.'

'No joke, sir.'

Another laugh. 'Ha! Okay then, this I have to see. Come on in.'

I chuckled to myself as we slowly meandered towards the house, the Merc making mincemeat of the thick snow that would have any other car stuck to the spot.

We stopped and Gregor got out, stylishly opened my door. Tom was standing at the entrance to the house, his mouth slightly ajar. 'Bloody hell, Dreamer,' he said as I approached. 'Smart suit and a Merc. What's going on?'

I tried to stay cool and ignored his question as I shook his hand. 'Is your gorgeous sister ready?' As the words left my mouth, the door opened slightly wider and Erika brushed past her brother. She wore a stunning black cocktail dress that flowed down to her knees and black, shiny high heels. A mini fur coat was draped over her shoulders to counter the icy temperatures.

I was in absolute awe of her presence. Her hair was immaculate. Her mellifluous blonde bob sat perfectly in place and brushed her jawline as she tilted her head slightly. She smiled at me; her lips tinted with a light pink balm and her small diamond earrings sparkled in the moonlight. Her stunning beauty took my breath away and my mouth became dry. She approached me smiling, her piercing green eyes hypnotising me into embarrassment.

'You look absolutely stunning,' I managed to say in one mushed-up sentence, leaning forward and kissing her on her cheek. She smelled exquisite, flowery.

'You don't look half bad yourself; I love the suit,' she giggled, linking my arm for our short walk to the car. 'Oh my goodness, is this car for us?'

I tried to play it down. 'Er … yes, it was part of the deal at La Maison.'

She looked up at me, grinned, and linked me a little tighter, giving me a tingle in my stomach.

'It still must be costing you a fortune.'

Gregor lifted his hat slightly and gave a small bow as he opened the door for us. Holding one of Erika's hands, I guided her into the car and she sat down, tucking her dress underneath her. She patted the seat next to her, encouraging me to sit. Obediently, I jumped at the request and perched myself comfortably next to her in the luxurious leather seat.

'Well, you couldn't have started any better, Mr Davidson. I'm rather impressed by your efforts so far.'

We chatted lightly in the back of the limo, and the journey to the hotel seemed to be over in an instant. Gregor drove the car around the side of the hotel towards the entrance of the restaurant.

'I've been dying to come here, huge bonus points for you on this one, Mark,' she said as she leaned forward slightly and glanced out of the window as we slowed to a stop.

The restaurant was normally filled with celebrities, actors, and the rich and famous. The food was rumoured to be world class, but it had a reputation of being ridiculously expensive.

Gregor opened our door and I got out, quickly turning to take Erika's hand and helping her out of the car. The door of the restaurant was opened by a pretty hostess, the maître d' hovering over us as we entered.

We were greeted by the restaurant manager, Madame Young. She was dressed in an immaculate blue suit, oozed charisma and her striking French accent was a pleasure to listen to.

'Monsieur Davidson, I presume?' she asked kindly.

'Yes, that's correct,' I answered, 'and this is Erika.'

'Pleased to meet you both. Now if you would care to follow me, your table is ready.'

'What the hell is going on?' Erika asked, looking at me with a little frown. 'How do they know you?'

I bumbled through a lie, that I had met some of the staff when I made the booking.

We followed Madame Young, Erika still linking me as we glanced around the amazing restaurant, then back at each other in awe.

Situated on two levels and fully lit with candlelight, all the tables were occupied, yet the atmosphere was calm and inviting. On the ground floor there were maybe a hundred tables, mostly couples or small groups, and a huge open-plan kitchen area towards the rear, where the finest chefs prepared and cooked the food.

The restaurant was decorated with a contemporary feel and some select local artists were exhibiting their work on various walls. Voted restaurant of the year in the UK for the past five years, it had just been given its third Michelin star and was, without question, the place to be for the rich and famous.

The first floor was an area for VIP guests and invited celebrities, allowing them to feel a sense of privacy and tranquillity.

We walked up the winding steps and onto the first level, passing diners as we headed to our table at the rear of the restaurant. 'Oh my God,' whispered Erika, 'there's Hugh Grant!'

'I hope he doesn't come to our table and ask for my autograph. Now that would just be embarrassing,' I joked as Erika giggled.

We sat in the booth facing each other as Madame Young placed our napkins over our knees. Our waitress handed over the menu as my face glowed ruby red and another waiter approached our table, placing an ice bucket at the side. 'As requested, sir, a bottle of number seventy-six. May I say a most excellent choice.'

He popped the cork without making a sound and poured Erika a small sample. 'Please,' he said and gestured his hand towards the glass. Erika looked at me excitedly and tasted the champagne.

'Wow, that's beautiful.'

'This is a fine champagne, mademoiselle, a '96 Louis Roederer Cristal Brut Rose Millesime.'

'Cristal champagne!' she exclaimed.

'Only the best for our first date,' I whispered.

She smiled and reached over, placing her left hand on top of mine. Convinced my face was glowing purple now, I linked one of my fingers over hers. This was only our first date, but everything felt so perfect. Oh, how my luck was changing.

12

The Plot Thickens

'The line is secure, sir. You may go ahead.'

Another two clicks and the divisional director took the lead, only this time there were just the two of them listening in.

'Reports?'

'There's been significant movement here in the UK. At least eight of his tags have moved into the northeast of England in the last twenty-four hours.'

Tags, members of the Tycoon's entourage had been given the aptly named code right at the beginning of the assignment. The Tycoon was number one on the MI6 most wanted list.

'Tracking?' he asked.

'Yes, sir. Each one has tracking. Where they go, we go.' Agent Gray smiled. She'd planned the whole manoeuvre from her laptop. She loved technology.

'Stay by your phone and I will let you know our friend's next movements. I'm leaving Moscow. He is on the move again.'

The phone went dead.

13

A First Kiss

We both selected our dishes and chatted for what seemed like hours, the conversation flowing effortlessly as the champagne took effect.

Playing a game, we would ask each other a question and then both answer it honestly. The subject varied from our first kiss to our favourite TV show and we learned more about each other in that first hour than you would normally learn in the first few months of dating.

Although we'd known each other as friends for many years, this was the first time we had learned intimate, private details about one another.

We were so alike it was actually quite eerie, learning that we loved the same music, the same types of food, the same types of movies and we both had a love for the south of France, convinced we would actually live there one day.

Erika had recently finished university after studying degrees in Law and Psychology. She was now taking a twelve-month break, wishing to travel before looking to start her career path. 'I could get used to doing nothing,' she said smiling, and took another sip of champagne.

'What about the travelling?' I asked. 'I would love to travel around the world, see different countries, mixed cultures, you know?'

'Absolutely, but it looks like budget, backpack travel for me. While Dad has a bob or two, I wouldn't expect him to fund me in lavish hotels. It's a tent and a sleeping bag for me, no fancy restaurants like this.'

I might just surprise you, I thought to myself.

She smiled and shrugged her shoulders, taking another sip of champagne, which by now was settling nicely into our bodies. 'I've always wanted to go to Vegas,' she said, 'the Grand Canyon, the casinos, the huge fancy hotels, but that's out of the question. I'd be spending my entire budget in a weekend.'

I smiled. 'There's nothing wrong with dreaming, Erika.'

'Absolutely, and if I win the lottery one day, I might consider taking you to repay you for tonight,' she said, winking at me.

Oh, the irony, I thought.

Our meal was outstanding; the steak I'd selected melted in my mouth while the second bottle of champagne was going down a treat. We finished our dessert and asked if we could be taken to the bar area for drinks to finish the night off in style.

Erika, like me, was a very tactile person and thought nothing of immediately holding my hands as we chatted, both of us leaning forward slightly and gazing into each other's eyes as our conversation flowed freely.

'Can I ask you a question?' I knew that my speech was a little slurred.

'Of course,' she said after a small hiccup.

I said it without thinking, the words just tumbled out of my mouth. 'I can't tell you how much I've enjoyed your company tonight.'

'That's not a question,' she said and laughed.

'Okay, the question is, may I kiss you?'

'You certainly cannot, Mr Davidson.'

I'd ruined the night. Jesus, why had I said that? Things were going so well.

And then she smiled wickedly. 'But I can kiss you.'

Before I had time to think, Erika leaned over the small table towards me and we kissed for the first time. It was better than I had imagined, soft and passionate, sensual and sexy as hell. I'd dreamed about this moment so many times, but my dream did not do it justice.

'Wow,' I said as we settled back into our seats.

'Wow,' replied Erika, smiling as she brushed her hair over her ears, looking slightly shy as we gazed at each other, her amazing eyes glistening in the table's candlelight.

'That was better than I ever imagined,' I said, taking another sip of champagne, my face once again red and flustered.

'How does this feel so, so right after only one night?' Erika asked as she stroked my hand. 'I'm never like this. I've never felt so comfortable with anyone.'

I reached out, touching her cheek. 'Me too. I know we've had a lot to drink, but I tend to speak the truth more when I am slightly intoxicated. It's like I've known this side of you forever.' As I finished the sentence I leaned over and kissed her again, longer and more passionately this time, my heart racing with excitement. We were completely unaware of our surroundings as we sat back in our seats, gazing into each other's eyes. It was at that moment that I knew I could quite easily fall in love with her. It was happening right here, right now. Regardless of time and regardless of how long we'd known each other in this capacity. I just knew in my heart that I was going to love her.

What a perfect end to what has surely turned out to be the best day of my life.

14

A Matter of National Security

Bert Simmons was the divisional director of MI6. The Secret Intelligence Service was the UK's external intelligence agency and was responsible for protecting British interests and security overseas, answerable to the Foreign and Commonwealth Office.

Simmons landed at Newcastle International Airport the very next morning, directly from Moscow.

The target was on his way to London. A team of agents had tracked him to the Hilton Hotel in London's Park Lane, where he would no doubt settle himself for the duration. Not too close to the action, but close enough to direct the operation.

At 39, Simmons was the youngest leader of Military Intelligence, Section 6, since its formation during the Second World War. After gaining his degree in criminology and psychology from Oxford University, the SIS had recruited him on graduation day and moved him quickly up the ranks.

Three years ago he was approached by the then retiring MI6 divisional director and told that he was being lined up for the job. The outgoing MI6 divisional director had one particular unresolved case on his books that he had worked on for more than a decade, and that was the 'Tycoon'.

He'd told Simmons that stopping the Tycoon and his operation was paramount to not only national, but world security. The man was running amok, his personal wealth was incalculable and he was now worth more than several Scandinavian nations. His secret stock holdings in the Russian stock market were close to 25%. He needed to be stopped sooner rather than later. It was just a matter of time before his criminal mind started influencing governments at the highest level.

'I think we should approach him,' Simmons said as soon as the conference call started. Sitting in the back of the stretched limo that collected him from the airport, he was more determined than ever to line up every duck in a row.

'I'm not sure that's a good idea, Bert.'

Harriet Minto was Simmons' right-hand woman, an Irish-American who'd made history as the only Irish woman to become a qualified judge before her thirtieth birthday. But within a few short months in the courtroom, she became bored and started to study criminal history and behavioural psychoanalysis as a way out.

Studying historical cases and how the world's most infamous criminals behaved captivated her to the point of obsession. The SIS had followed her career closely for nearly two years and eventually made their move and offered her a way out of the courtroom.

Will Thomas was the newest member of the team. 'I think she's right, Bert. Surely making him aware of the situation would make him far too nervous and arouse suspicion with the Tags?' Will was quickly becoming the sensible, middle-ground member of the SIS senior team.

'I know you're both right of course. It's the jet lag, it brings out the desperate side of me. Let's stick to the plan and let things unfold. We've learned plenty from the others and each time he becomes more predictable. This is our time. I can feel it.'

'There's one more thing, Bert,' Minto said.

'Yes?'

'His Number Two has slapped himself directly into the story and already made contact.'

15

Oblivious to the World

For the next two days and nights, Erika and I stayed in and around the hotel. Apart from the occasional calls to home and friends, we stayed in suite 401, oblivious to the outside world.

At the end of our first date and three bottles of champagne later, I told Erika that my 'deal' included a night in the hotel.

'I don't want you to leave,' I had blurted out as we finished the third bottle and contemplated calling it a night. She told me she didn't want to leave and we had stumbled upstairs, giggling like two naughty teenagers.

Our first night alone together was not the sexy, eventful evening I'd hoped it would be, but was perfect all the same.

After throwing our clothes off all over the room, we jumped into the huge bed in the darkness. I'd left a window open; the room was freezing cold and as we huddled together inside the crispy sheets, we embraced each other to keep warm. It was so comfortable and felt so perfect lying in each other's arms. We were both intoxicated and fell sound asleep like two babies.

The next morning, I'd woken up to find Erika already awake, stroking my hair as she lay close to me.

'Hey you,' I said, leaning towards her and kissing her soft lips.

'Hey you,' she replied.

It was then, for the first time, that the light kiss turned into a passionate kiss, and finally my dreams were about to be fulfilled as we edged closer to each other, my heart rate tripling in an instant.

I held her naked body in my arms, pressing together as we kissed deeply. I felt her breasts press against my chest, which turned me on instantly, and as I kissed her neck softly, my hands moved seductively down her back as she bit my ear, moaning gently.

Her leg arched over my hip, inviting me to touch her as I returned to her soft lips and kissed her tenderly. My hands caressed her perfectly shaped behind as she found my hand and led me down towards her, eager for me to feel how much she wanted me.

As I touched her she moaned at me, gripping my hair gently, and whispered that she wanted to feel me inside her. I needed no encouragement. I was so turned on at that point and wanted nothing more than to be experiencing what I'd only ever dreamed of so many times before.

She pulled me on top of her, smiling as our two bodies became one. The euphoric feeling of making love to this beautiful girl sent shivers down the length of my spine. I knew, without question, I wanted to spend the rest of my life with her. This was no fling or a one-night stand. As we made passionate love together, holding each other closely, I was elated at how my life had flipped over the last twenty-four hours.

On the third day she started asking questions. By now she was curious where all the money was coming from. I think she'd seen the wine list and the hotel and its prices were listed on their website.

I gave her the brush-off, lied about a fake competition and a deal, said I was more than happy to put a hole in my redundancy payment because 'she was worth every penny'.

'I don't want this to end,' I whispered as we woke up on the morning of our last day at the hotel.

'Me neither,' she replied, kissing me tenderly, resting her head on my chest.

'Let's go away together for a holiday.'

She sat up with a serious look on her face. 'And where do you suggest?'

'Anywhere. Somewhere warmer than this bloody country, the best hotels, we could fly first class.'

She slipped out of bed, pulled on a robe, her smile fading for the first time in three days. As she brushed her hair, she turned and faced me. 'Are you serious, Mark?'

'Absolutely I am. You just tell me where you'd like to go.'

'Don't joke, Mark. I've an idea how much your redundancy payment was and I have no intention of letting you blow that on a holiday.'

Should I just tell her about the money? I'd vowed that I'd tell my family first. In my own time, when everything had calmed down. I stood watching her. I realised at that point in time that I loved her with all my heart. I could trust her, I know I could. It would eat away at me if I kept this a secret from her now.

'My brother said you were a dreamer,' she laughed.

The words hurt a little. I frowned and stared longingly into her eyes.

Quickly, she continued. 'But you need to be practical, otherwise your money will run out. I'd love to go on holiday with you, why don't we consider backpacking? We could do it on a budget.'

And at that very moment, I knew that her feelings for me didn't revolve around money. But sleeping in tents and fields and living on boiled rice and pulses held no appeal for me.

She sat on the bed and kissed me again. 'Dreamer ...'

I stroked her hair once more and then ... 'I've got something to tell you,' I said before she had chance to finish her sentence.

'Please don't tell me you have a girlfriend.' She sat upright.

'Oh my God, no, nothing like that.'

A sense of relief settled on Erika's face and I continued. 'These last three days have been the most exciting and enjoyable of my entire life. I feel you know everything there possibly is to know about me. That is ... almost everything.'

She started looking confused, clearly trying to gather her thoughts.

'I think the easiest way to do this is to just show you.' I jumped off the bed and walked over to my briefcase. 'You need to see this.'

I pulled out the bank transfer statement and handed it to her. My heart was pounding as she opened the statement and then looked at me. She looked at the statement again and then back at me. 'I, but I don't understand? That's … that's just not possible. How, what, how is that even …?' She stumbled through the sentence, unable to register what she was reading. 'This is your bank account, your money?'

'Yes.'

16

Letting the Cat out of the Bag

Erika was completely blown away, still not saying much. I told her about my aversion to sleeping in tents and told her that a holiday anywhere in the world could be the starting point to our long-term relationship. 'We are both free. We have no ties, so let's jump on Google and look at some hotels.'

She nodded. 'Yes … yes … just a week. Let's see what happens.'

And then … 'But how, Mark, how can you possibly have that much money?'

A deep breath. The time was right. Erika would be the first person to know.

'I won the lottery, Erika. I won two hundred and forty-five million Pounds. It was the lottery office who booked me into the hotel.

An eerie silence floated in the air for a few seconds before she burst into life. 'Are you kidding me? I ... I... what, oh my God, Mark, I don't know what to say!'

'You're the only person who knows Erika and I've signed legal documents that prevent the lottery from releasing my name. The worst thing I think I could do right now would be to go public or to even tell my parents, especially while the press is on the prowl.'

'Your parents don't know?'

'No. My parents always wanted a simple, quiet life, and now me, throwing that kind of curveball? I couldn't do it. I think it's best to wait, there's no rush, my parents are financially stable and are happy with their lives. Why turn their world upside down?'

A silence followed. Erika sat on the bed, unable to comprehend what I'd just told her. I let it sink in.

I reached for her hand. 'Let me take you to some of the places you have always dreamed of. We can get away from this awful weather and grab some sun, maybe have a little fun for a few weeks while all the media hype dies down.'

'Really,' she replied, 'do you think we should?'

'What's stopping us? It's freezing here and I know it's almost Christmas, but all of this snow, I've had enough of it. I want sunshine, cocktails, casinos, and the company of the most beautiful girl in the world. Say you'll come with me?'

She leaped into the air. 'Of course, of course, I'll come with you!'

She jumped on the bed and I joined her and we started bouncing. We jumped up and down on the bed like two excited kids, throwing our hands in the air, laughing out loud and screaming, lost in the euphoria of happiness.

We spent the rest of the morning with our heads buried in laptops, surfing the net and working out the practicalities.

I settled the bill and we checked out.

I thought it best to play it low key with the family. We took a taxi to my parents' house and we told them we were heading off for a Christmas break but didn't say where. We did the same with Tom and Erika's parents. Everyone seemed delighted for us.

I left Erika to pack a couple of cases and told her I'd give her a call later, then headed back to the hotel. I still had one last thing to do.

I found Bob in his office.

'Good morning, sir. I hope you enjoyed your stay?'

'Bob, I had an absolute ball, I can't thank you enough for your help,' I said, shaking his hand. 'Tell me, can you spare me ten minutes of your time? Can I get you a coffee in the bar?'

Bob looked at me inquisitively. 'Why certainly, sir.'

The waitress brought two coffees and I cleared my throat. 'I can't thank you enough for all your help, Bob, and I'd like to ask you a question, if I may?'

'A question? Of course, sir.'

'How would you like a job?' I said.

'A job, sir? What kind of job?

'I need an assistant. Not full time, just someone to help me when I need some things organised, a PA, like those executives have. With your vast knowledge and experience, I can't think of anyone more qualified.'

'I … well, I don't know, sir, I've been doing this job for quite a while now, and well, at my age I guess I need to be careful. It's a steady job and pays well.'

I wasn't going to take no for an answer. 'Hear me out Bob, I need someone to help me make bookings, travel arrangements, and assist in purchasing goods, things like that, just like you've done for me over the last few days. You can work from home. I'll sort you out with a mobile phone and a laptop; All of your duties can be carried out while you work from home, meaning you can care for your wife at the same time.'

I allowed the dust to settle as Bob's mind raced, no doubt filled with questions. 'You don't need to give me an answer now. Just promise me you'll think about it.'

I opened my briefcase and handed him a cheque for five thousand Pounds. 'This is a thank you for all of your help over the last few days.'

He looked stunned. 'Mr Davidson, I cannot accept this, please, it is too much.'

'Bob, you've earned it. Get it in the bank today and buy your wife something nice for Christmas. I have special clearance, so the funds will transfer immediately. Think about my offer and call me soon because I have a few things to organise.' I patted him on the shoulder as I turned towards the door. 'Oh, and by the way, your salary will be fifty thousand pounds a year.' I opened the door and Bob jumped from the chair. He stopped me in my tracks.

'Are you serious, sir?'

'I am.'

Bob told me he would start right away. He said that kind of money was more than his wife and he could have ever hoped for. 'Bless you, sir, you have a kind heart.' His eyes were moist.

'And from now on you call me Mark, okay, none of this "sir" shit.'

'Yes, Mark,' he beamed.

I passed him a list of things to do. 'You'd better get moving Bob, I need a few things organised pretty quickly if you're up to it.'

He quickly scanned the list and smiled. 'I'm on the case.'

Three hours later, as I collected Erika in a taxi, heading for Newcastle Airport, Bob called with an update. He had booked a private charter jet for our trip. It was due to depart later that evening and we'd spend the next few hours in the VIP executive lounge. The Hawker 4000 was a mid-sized business jet and the ultimate in luxury travel, comprising such items as heated reclining leather chairs, wide-screen TVs, private waitress service, and even a double bed. The jet was large enough for twelve passengers and would land at Newcastle International Airport, refuel and take off with just two passengers on board.

We would fly directly to New York City for one night, staying at the world-renowned Plaza Hotel, overlooking Central Park. The presidential suite was a lavish fifteen thousand pounds for one night, offering a private butler and chef, five bedrooms, a wine cellar, and our own personal chauffeur. We would enjoy a private shopping experience at one of the huge department stores, stay overnight and then fly to Las Vegas on Christmas Day.

Bob had made a reservation at the exclusive Bellagio Villas in Las Vegas for sixteen nights. It was a snip at only six thousand dollars per night. My request for one of the most expensive villas in Las Vegas got us a huge, private villa with six oversized bedrooms and no fewer than seven bathrooms. With a private pool and terrace area as well as our own butler and limousine for the entire trip, it was extravagance at its finest.

After our sixteen days of luxury, we would fly to Miami, spending the night at The Setai on South Beach, where a whopping thirty thousand dollars bought us one night in the penthouse suite.

Finally, we would return to the UK the next day, arriving at Heathrow and taking a limousine into London, where we had a booking at the Dorchester Hotel. The Harlequin suite cost a mere six thousand pounds a night. It was made famous by Elizabeth Taylor as the very suite where she received the news of her record-breaking deal to star in the epic Cleopatra.

I was about to spend a huge amount of money.

The thought made me shiver but imagining Erika's face on this holiday would be worth every penny. All I had to remember was that during the full 19-day trip, I would earn six hundred thousand pounds in interest payments, so the trip would actually earn me money rather than be at my expense. It hardly seemed fair.

Part One of my plan was complete, and it had taken Bob less than two hours to secure everything through his network of contacts. This told me he was worth every penny of investment and would be an exceptionally worthwhile asset for the future.

Over the last few days, while I was locked away in the hotel with Erika, my winnings had been fully transferred to my new bank account. The only money I'd spent so far was around eighty thousand Pounds, and I've earned way more than that in interest. Even booking lavish hotels, private jets, and the most ridiculous amount of spending money, I was still making a profit, which just seemed crazy. But who was I to argue with the bank?

I kept a record of my purchase history and printed a bank balance every day to keep track. I made a mental note to arrange my own accountant when I returned and knew the exact person for the job. My good friend Si was always complaining about long hours at his accountancy firm, so what better way for him to step up the career path than to open his own accountancy firm with one special client, his good friend Mark Davidson? But that was a conversation for later.

It was in the VIP lounge of the airport that everything started to sink in and I realised I wasn't locked in a dream after all. Dreams didn't last this long. Erika looked radiant, a permanent smile plastered across her face.

I drifted back to our time together over the past few days. It was pretty incredible how we hit it off so quickly. It was hard to describe how happy I felt when I was with her, or even when I thought about her. This was a feeling I'd never experienced, and I had to admit that I loved it. My past girlfriends had never really sparked a reaction like this and I guess working for the telecoms company, usually six days a week, I'd never had time for a real relationship.

But Erika was someone special and maybe it was the fact that I'd wanted this to happen for so long that made me feel this way. I promised myself I would always treat her like a princess, but at the same time try to keep things in perspective. But with two hundred and forty-five million pounds in the bank, it was easier said than done.

17

An American Friend

Bob called me on my mobile at around 8 p.m. with a further update on the rest of my list and the flight details of the private charter jet. The gift that I'd asked him to assist with had proved quite a challenge but, after five hours of continuous phone calls and emails, he managed to secure my request. There would be some paperwork to complete, which he had already emailed over to me and I would need to make a payment tonight.

'Bob, you have exceeded my expectations,' I said, thanking him for all of his time and efforts.

'My pleasure and might I take this opportunity to wish you and your family a happy Christmas. My wife passes on her appreciation and says having me home full time was the best present anyone could give. I will be by the phone if you need me, sir.'

'Bob, I shouldn't need you for the next few weeks, so take some time off with your wife and enjoy the holidays. Have a great Christmas.'

My mobile phone rang again, interrupting my train of thought and the 15-digit number told me it was a call from the United States. On my way to my parents' house, I'd placed a call to an old contact from the telecoms business. Before leaving, I signed an enormous deal for the company which I was very well rewarded for, and over the two-year period of negotiations, I made some great new friends in the USA.

One of the guys I'd become really close to and had stayed in regular contact with told me about a huge business deal he was involved in just as I was leaving. They were about to secure some major investment for an exciting, secret project and I'd not spoken to him for a while.

I'd visited him at various stages of the contract negotiations at his Los Angeles offices and built up a great working relationship, which was one reason we had won the contract so easily. We'd spent many hours partying on my company's entertainment budget and had become great friends.

Now seemed like an ideal time to find out how he had progressed. He was hopefully returning my call to give me the gory details. The call would also give me some exciting news that would be timed very nicely with my trip to the States.

18

Winner on the Move

Minto called Simmons at his hotel in the early hours of the morning. 'Sir, things have taken a bit of a turn.'

'What's happened?' Simmons was half asleep, the jetlag clearly taking its toll.

'He's going to Vegas.'

'Who's going to bloody Vegas?'

'The winner, Davidson, he's booked on a private jet to New York and then on to Vegas. It leaves in a couple of hours.'

'You have to be shitting me.'

'Afraid not, Bert. However, I have managed to plant one of our team onto the flight attendant roster. It's Christmas time and not many people volunteer for these things.'

'Well done, Minto. I'm getting up, we need to book—'

'Already done, sir. We are booked on the 11 a.m. flight directly to Vegas. And we have a team already on their way to New York.'

'Way ahead of the curve, as usual. See you in a few hours.'

19

Hawker 4000

A man in a smart suit approached us in the VIP lounge. 'Mr Davidson, could you follow me? Your flight is almost ready. I'll take you through check-in, no need for those formalities.'

'Take us through check-in?' Erika quizzed.

'I think Bob has sorted it. No waiting around for us.' I shrugged, stretching the truth slightly as we approached an airport attendant holding a plaque with my name on it. The reality was that it had cost me an arm and a leg. Money talks, it seems that rich people don't need to bother with the usual search and security issues.

'Mr Davidson, very pleased to meet you, sir. My name is Helen. Please leave your cases here. My colleague will take them through check-in and directly to the aircraft for you.'

'That's very kind,' I said, handing over our cases.

'Let's get inside,' she said. 'The weather is not the greatest and I'm sure you're keen to get settled.'

We followed her through the airport where hundreds of festive holiday makers were packed in abundance, checking in their luggage, going through security and preparing to leave for the holidays. We continued through the main concourse to the rear of the airport until we reached a small check-in area marked Private Flights Only.

Within two minutes, we had checked in and followed the attendant through a dedicated, private area of the airport I had never seen before.

Walking hand in hand and giggling like children, we arrived at Private Gate A, Erika still blissfully unaware of the experience we were about to undertake.

I spotted the Hawker 4000 on the runway, just outside of the glass window. It was a beautiful sight, one I had seen many times in airports and wished that I could just see the inside, never mind becoming a passenger.

'Just down the staircase through here,' Helen pointed. 'We will have you on board in a few moments.'

As we walked down the steps and onto the tarmac towards the plane, Erika's face was changed in an instant.

Helen turned around. 'If you would care to board via the steps at the front, the captain will meet you inside.'

'Oh my God,' Erika said and froze at the bottom of the steps. 'Are you kidding me?'

I smiled at her as she gripped my hand tightly with her mouth still partially open, we climbed the small stairway to where the captain and a flight attendant were waiting to greet us.

'Good morning, my name is Phil Wilson and I'm your captain. Welcome on-board your personal jet.'

My heart was racing with excitement, desperate to see inside the luxurious liner.

'Sir, madam,' the captain continued, 'she will be your transport for the next few days. This is the senior cabin manager, Caroline Bisset, and she will be here to take care of you both during the flight.'

He touched the side of his head with his finger, saluting us, and motioned towards our hostess. She was young, maybe early twenties, but very professional, and smiled at us politely as we boarded. I had to admit that I was utterly stunned at the jet's lavish beauty.

The first thing I noticed were the seats. They were huge, cream leather recliners, oozing comfort and style. There was a small bar area at the front of the plane and no less than three wide-screen TVs placed around the cabin. Towards the rear of the jet was a sleeping area, a washroom and even a small meeting area for serious business meetings.

The captain spoke again. 'We have fifteen minutes before take-off, so if you'd like to take your seats, please. Once we are airborne, Caroline will give you the grand tour. Please have an enjoyable flight and I will keep you updated from the cockpit as to our progress.'

He left us as we excitedly took our seats in the large chairs, clicking our belts into place. I grabbed Erika's hand just as the engines fired up to taxi us to the runway. Whoever said money cannot buy happiness was clearly extremely poor.

20

The Club

After an ultra-smooth take-off, we were given the tour of our own piece of heaven.

Starting at the rear was the sleeping area, which had a comfortable-looking double bed and a bathroom with its own shower. Outside the bedroom, the meeting area had a large mahogany standalone desk, two computers hooked up to video calling, touch screen TVs and weirdly a 1990's style fax machine.

Towards the middle of the jet was the lounge, which opened out into a seating area for 12 passengers, each with its own oversized recliner. The walls were made from shiny, dark brown walnut, oozing style and expense. Finally, there was a white suede sofa facing a large TV screen leading towards the cockpit. All in all, pretty impressive to say the least and best of all, it belonged to us for the next two days.

The flight took a lengthy eight hours and while drinking champagne a few hours into the flight, I'd informed Erika we were stopping off for a night on the way.

'New York!' she screamed, clearly thrilled at the detour.

'I can think of nothing better than spending Christmas Day with you in the presidential suite in of the world's most famous hotel in the middle of New York City, overlooking a snow-filled Central Park,' I said, raising my glass for a toast.

'I cannot believe this is happening,' she replied, smiling. She sat on my lap as we sipped our champagne. 'It's just like a dream.'

'I have an idea,' I said with a wicked grin. 'There's a club I'd like us to join.'

'Really?' She said in all innocence. 'Which club is that?'

'We'll need to go through the membership details. They are in the bedroom at the back of the plane.'

21

Checking in

Bissett picked up the phone and dialled. She waited a few seconds. 'Sir,' she said, 'we will land in New York in around two hours. No unusual activity, just two love birds on an exciting trip to New York and Las Vegas.'

'Stay close and if you hear any changes to their agenda, call me.'

'I will, sir.'

Simmons was already in the air and heading for Las Vegas.

22

New York

Because of the time difference, it was mid-afternoon when we landed in New York and, rather than going straight to the hotel, we decided to go shopping.

The hotel limo collected us from the airport and after a small discussion with the driver, we were on our way to Bloomingdales, home of the 'little brown bag' and seven and a half floors of shopping heaven.

Clearly Erika was overjoyed at the prospect of shopping, whereas I just wanted to fill my suitcase with enough clothes for our trip and head straight back to the hotel. Even though we were in the Big Apple, I'd seen enough snow to last me a lifetime and would have preferred to watch the current blizzard from our lavish hotel room.

As we walked into Bloomingdales, our personal shoppers were waiting to escort us around the store to assist with purchasing.

'What more can you ask for?' I said, as we met our hosts. I glanced at Erika. She was looking unsure and I knew exactly what was going through her head. 'Erika, this is my present to you. Don't go looking at the price tags, do you hear me? If you like it, then get it.'

'But … I can't, it wouldn't be right.'

'Money is no object for the next sixteen days. And if it makes you feel any better, you can work out the monthly interest I earn.'

That last statement seemed to do the trick. She wasn't stupid, even if she'd worked the interest out at a nominal rate of 2.5%, she'd have calculated a figure that was quite incomprehensible.

I watched as she disappeared towards the lift with her assistant leading the way.

Two hours disappeared in an instant and I frightened myself at how addictive shopping with no budget could be. When we both arrived at the same time at Bloomingdales show-time café on floor 7½, our personal attendants were laden with bags and boxes.

Erika's was smiling.' Just … wow. I could live in this store. I just wanted everything I laid my eyes on.'

'Me too,' I replied, laughing.

'I'm afraid I needed to buy another suitcase. I'm sorry,' she said, blinking her hypnotically beautiful eyes at me.

'Don't apologise and besides, I needed to buy another one too. I told you, you don't need to worry about it. I will make more on this holiday in interest than we could ever spend in this store and I know it made you happy, right?'

'Yes, but it still feels, I don't know, strange.'

'I don't think that feeling will ever go away.'

New York was covered in snow, the famous skyscrapers adorned with bright festive lights that made the city look stunning. It was extraordinarily busy with shoppers and holidaymakers. Everyone seemed to have a festive glow about them. Christmas in New York was a special time and as we sat in the back of the limo, watching people rushing about their business, I felt completely overwhelmed. Erika glanced at me as if to read my mind, smiling without saying a word.

We arrived at the exclusive Plaza Hotel on the world-renowned 5th Avenue, often classed as the 'most expensive street in the world'. The hotel has over two hundred and eighty distinctive guestrooms, including over one hundred suites, and boasts the largest square footage of any luxury hotel in New York City. Money couldn't buy better than our accommodation for the evening.

Bob had made the call to the hotel to arrange our booking in one of the suites and the receptionist had mentioned that actor Mickey Rourke had cancelled the Royal Plaza Suite due to severe weather conditions. They told Bob it was the best suite in the hotel and as they were unlikely to fill it at this late stage, they were only too pleased to offer it to us at a reduced rate.

I can't describe the overwhelming feeling of joy and elation I felt as we entered the room via our own, private elevator. The suite was almost five thousand square feet, with three enormous king-size bedrooms, three large bathrooms and our own secluded area overlooking the spectacular views of Manhattan, Fifth Avenue and the legendary Pulitzer Fountain.

We were both a little shell-shocked at the sheer scale of everything. Why on earth did we need all that space? However, that was irrelevant and I reminded Erika that it had been significantly reduced, so who were we to argue?

A series of unique oval and round vestibules connected the suite's formal entertainment rooms, which included an exquisitely designed living room featuring a white grand piano. A large butler's pantry and a professional kitchen facilitates sophisticated entertaining and we also had the services of a personal chef. The gymnasium with state-of-the-art fitness equipment appealed to me as I'd not had a workout in over a week.

In short, we had died and gone to hotel heaven and it took us a while to finally utter a few words to each other.

Finally, Erika said, 'I've never seen anything like this in my life.' She gazed around the huge living room overlooking 5th Avenue.

'Me neither. I think my entire apartment block would fit in here.'

'I can't believe we'll be here on Christmas Day,' she said, 'it's the most beautiful setting I have ever seen in my life. I can't believe it, I just can't.'

Erika strolled over to me and grabbed my hand, leading me towards the shiny, white grand piano. She climbed on the top of it, opening her legs and wrapping them around my waist, and kissed me. The whole day had been such an overwhelming experience, and it took us over rapidly.

Without a second thought to anything or anyone and in complete view of Central Park, I removed Erika's clothes, gently peeling the pieces off and dropping them onto the floor. Leaning forward and sitting on the edge of the piano, she removed my T-shirt. As she removed the rest of my clothes, our kisses became deeper and more urgent. I was shaking slightly, still nervous by her presence and utterly overwhelmed by her beauty.

I ran my fingers through her soft, silky hair. 'I think I'm falling in love with you,' I whispered into her ear. I felt slightly embarrassed that I had just blurted it out in the heat of the moment.

'Oh Mark, I think I love you too,' she whispered, easing forwards on the piano, her moistness teasing me and her hands stroking my back. 'Make love to me,' she begged, lying backwards on top of the piano, grabbing my hands and teasingly placing them on her breasts.

I didn't need to be asked twice and as I guided myself towards her and slowly entered her, the world around us vanished. I was lost in beauty and I knew that I would never experience happiness or pleasure like this. The money, the expensive and lavish lifestyle, the private jets and the fancy hotels – I'd give it all up if I could spend the rest of my days with this girl.

Our chef had prepared an exquisite dinner of bison filet and sautéed vegetables and we dined in the living room, which was festively decorated with tinsel and candles.

There was a magnificent twelve-foot, white Christmas tree in the corner of the room opposite the piano, which glistened with bright, twinkling tree lights; the room glowing slightly.

We sat together on the large sofa, enjoying our food in our oversized robes after a long soak in the gargantuan corner bath. A little classical music played in the background, and a perfectly selected French merlot complemented the magnificent meal. We kept smiling at each other, glancing around the room in disbelief.

Central Park was bursting with Christmas décor and although we'd come on holiday to leave the snow behind, as we sat hand in hand gazing out of the full height window into the blustery darkness and the artificial lights caught the snowflakes as they drifted from the sky, I sensed it was as close to heaven that I was ever likely to get.

23

Vegas-bound

'Merry Christmas, babe,' Erika whispered into my ear as I opened my eyes to see her stunning face glancing at me.

'Merry Christmas, gorgeous,' I replied, kissing her gently and smiling as I sat up and it dawned on me where we were.

'This is for you.' She handed me a perfectly wrapped silver box, with a silver bow placed on top.

'For me?'

'It's just a small gift for Christmas Day, that's all,' she replied. 'After everything you've done for me, our trip away, a ridiculous shopping trip, just ... well, everything. I got you this at home and thought it would be nice to give you today.' She smiled.

I slowly pulled at the silver wrapping paper to reveal a plain white box. I looked at her inquisitively, raising one eyebrow.

'Is it a new pair of shoes?' I asked, holding the box up to my eye level. It was about the size of a mobile phone and fairly light to hold.

I inched open the box and to my sheer delight, found a beautiful, silver, Tag Heuer watch lodged into the foam shaped centre.

'Look at the back,' she said, pulling out the watch and handing it to me. 'I hope you like it.'

I turned the watch around and inscribed on the back was a small message which read:

Mark & Erika, Simply Fate

'Wow, I love it.' I was overcome with emotion. The words inscribed on the back described our growing relationship perfectly. 'But you're not getting off lightly,' I said as I jumped out of bed and rushed over to my suitcase. I located the box which had been delivered to the hotel yesterday, just as planned. I'd told Erika that I needed to do some paperwork for our stay and had sneaked to reception and collected it. 'Happy Christmas,' I said, climbing back into bed.

'You didn't need to get me a present. You've already given me so much.'

'It's Christmas Day, you can't be in New York City on Christmas Day and not have a present to open, can you?'

I handed her the small box, wrapped perfectly with a petite silky bow.

'Thank you so much,' she said, smiling, as she removed the bow, taking a deep breath and looking a little nervous as she opened it.

The light blue box from the store that I ordered it from was an immediate giveaway. Tiffany & Co boxes have a unique colour, recognisable anywhere.

'Oh, oh my God … is, is that a blue diamond?'

'Yeah,' I replied. 'I hope you like it.'

'Like it? Oh my God, Mark. I … that's… oh my God…' She tried to keep the sentence together but failed, her eyes welling up with tears.

The necklace itself was platinum and housed a 1.25 carat, oval shaped blue diamond. It was one of the world's rarest diamonds. It was simple yet elegant and an absolute steal at only sixty thousand dollars. The look on her face made it worth every American cent.

Placing our gifts on the side of the bed, we lay in each other's arms and as natural as night follows day, we made passionate love, as a Xmas orchestra played *White Christmas* softly on the radio.

What a perfect start to Christmas morning.

The streets were almost empty as we were driven to New York's JFK airport the next morning in the hotel's embarrassingly large black limousine.

Our Christmas Day afternoon had been spent sampling at the hotel's new champagne bar, where we'd purchased a bottle of 1996 Dom Pérignon Rosé.

After the bubbles started to take effect, Erika had dared me to try the Special Reserve Ossetra caviar. Money may buy the finer things in life, but I would preferred one of the hot dogs from the famous New York vendors outside to a bowl of malodorous, overpriced fish eggs.

We'd both called home to wish the family a happy Christmas, telling them a slight variation of the truth about our time.

'Make sure you stay in touch,' my mum had said, 'and make sure you are both careful. There are gangsters in America and they have guns.'

Too many movies, mother … 'Don't worry, Mum. We'll be fine.'

I had settled the bill when my American friend and colleague called to update me on his whereabouts and confirmed he would meet up with me in Las Vegas in a few days' time. Everything was starting to fall into place perfectly.

Thirty minutes later, we were aboard Katie, our private jet.

The same pilot, co-pilot and air hostess, Caroline, had stayed over in New York and were back again for the journey to Las Vegas.

'Really appreciate you working over Christmas,' I said to Caroline as we settled into our seats.

'It's really no problem, sir.' She locked the door and took her seat.

As soon as the jet was in the air, and the seatbelt signs switched off, Caroline was on her feet and asked us what we wanted to drink. It was all rather predictable now. 'Champagne please,' we chorused, giggling like two small children.

After the second bottle, we were both feeling quite lightheaded and I slept the remainder of the flight.

24

As planned

Some hours later, Bissett took a seat at the rear of the plane and picked up the phone. 'Everything is as planned, sir,' she said. 'We will approach Vegas within the hour and they plan to head straight to the villa.'

'Everything cool?'

'Yes, sir.'

Bissett had spent the night in the same hotel as the happy couple, although the mediocre room was a far cry from their penthouse suite.

She observed from a dark corner as they happily drank champagne and wished she could be that content with someone. It was like watching a romantic Hollywood movie. It was a lonely job working at MI6, but she had made her bed and, in truth, she loved every second.

25

Bellagio

The limo collected us from the airport and in less than twenty minutes we arrived at the luxurious Bellagio Villas. The snow and icy temperatures were now a distant memory, as the temperature in Vegas had increased to a modest 30°C.

An attendant from the Bellagio was waiting to greet us as we departed the limo and he unloaded our cases onto an awaiting trolley. The main hotel itself was utterly breath-taking, and we arrived just as the fountains were on full display. Hundreds of people were gathered around the entrance, watching in wonder as the water shot up into the air in perfect sequence to music, together with a light display that matched perfectly.

'It's magnificent,' said Erika as we strolled past the front of the main hotel to the rear of the complex.

We were staying in one of the largest villas at the resort and wow, was this a glorious sight. It was over eight thousand square feet of supreme luxury and had a gymnasium, a private massage room, dry sauna, a hair salon, private kitchen area, formal dining room, a fully stocked bar, and a gorgeous private terrace which led to a quaint garden that housed a hidden private swimming pool and Jacuzzi.

A classic European décor gave it a homely, familiar feel.

The butler left our cases at the door as we rushed around the villa, exploring every room and utterly jubilant at the prospect of spending more than two whole weeks in complete luxury.

The exclusive Picasso Restaurant was booked for 8 p.m. Erika wore a simple pink dress, light blue shoes and a blue bag that went perfectly with the blue diamond necklace around her neck. She was not your typical girl who spent hours in front of a mirror, which suited me perfectly. She radiated natural beauty and did not need any makeup for her to look exquisite. 'You look amazing,' I said as we left the villa.

The restaurant had a variety of replica Picassos and one or two original masterpieces hanging on the walls. An impressive collection of charming ceramic pieces, to further delight the senses of diners enjoying the Picasso experience, were in various corners around the room. With soaring cove ceilings, intimate nooks and brilliant bursts of flowers, it was a dream of country elegance.

We spent the next few hours eating fantastic food, washing it down with a bottle of 1999 Le Pin Pomerol. We chatted about our plans for the next few weeks and grew excited at the prospect of amusing ourselves in the casino later.

The Bellagio Casino had everything, and I could easily see how so many people became addicted to gambling in Vegas. Part of me wanted to race onto the floor and start placing chips immediately, but I needed to be sensible and not get too lost in the moment.

I ordered a bottle of Moët and we meandered over to the roulette tables. I decided to watch for a while before selecting our game table.

There were hundreds of people from of all walks of life milling around the poker tables, betting anything from one dollar to one hundred thousand dollars at a time. It was astonishing how much money was being spent and I vowed not to be lured in by the pretence that this lifestyle was just a game. Back home in the UK the only time I would ever visit a casino was at the end of a night out with the boys, spending a maximum of twenty Pounds. I normally lost it within ten minutes.

26

Highs and Lows

'I think they're being followed.' Bissett had been perched at a roulette table close by. 'There were two of them watching, one at the craps table and the other sat at the bar.'

She had become an expert in surveillance techniques and could quickly identify anyone surveying an area.

'Where are they now?' Simmons asked.

'They just left the casino. Minto is on their tail and I'm about to head over to their villa to plant the bugs.'

'Switch. Minto, get over to the villa and get those bugs planted. Bissett, follow them and keep your eyes peeled to the two tags. It would be completely out of character if they tried anything with this many people around, but we need to be prepared for anything.'

27

All that glitters

Our first night of gambling had been rather successful.

After splitting a ton of casino chips with Erika and selecting our roulette table for the evening, she correctly selected the winning numbers twice in a row and had won a tidy sum in the first twenty minutes. She continued her winning streak and was sitting next to me with over one thousand five hundred dollars in chips within an hour. A great night's work for anyone, and she was utterly delighted.

I, on the other hand, had lost a thousand dollars in about two minutes before my luck changed as I selected the winning number three times in a row.

Our luck continued and we were on our second bottle of champagne when Erika had won an unbelievable eight thousand dollars. She could not believe her luck and our spirits were high.

But now I was getting bored, and I needed some fresh air. I placed every chip I had, spread between just three numbers. I wasn't even paying attention as the croupier spun the ball and, as a great cheer rose from the table, I wondered what all the fuss was about.

The ball had landed on my number, netting me just shy of one hundred and ninety thousand dollars.

Funny that when you have money, it somehow always turns into more money.

We decided to take a walk around the huge fountains outside the hotel, stretch our legs, and soak in the atmosphere. Using my phone's map, we meandered down the main strip, turning right out of the hotel, towards Planet Hollywood.

The Vegas strip was astonishing, full of lights, glitz, and a feel-good party atmosphere. It was way into the early hours of the morning, yet there was no sign of this city sleeping as thousands of people milled around, spilling out onto the roads as the odd car or two slowly manoeuvred their way around the bodies.

As we moseyed up towards Planet Hollywood, we noticed the Paris section on our left-hand side and headed towards the fully lit, miniature Eiffel Tower, which looked dazzling in the distance.

Erika was starting to struggle in her high heels, so she removed them and walked barefoot across the road towards the tower. The mixture of cool air and champagne was starting to affect me. I found a small alleyway, and we sat on a wooden bench, to get our bearings and give Erika's feet a rest from the road.

'I hope the tower has an elevator,' Erika joked as we gazed at the brightly lit monument.

'Yeah me too.' I laughed, the alcohol clearly taking its toll on our fitness levels.

Erika and I had been chatting for a few moments and had decided to leave and head towards the tower.

As she stood up from the bench, I'd bent over to fasten my laces and out of nowhere, two men sheepishly approached us. The taller man took no prisoners as he kicked me full on in the ribcage and knocked me to the ground. The pain was excruciating. At the same time, his accomplice moved in towards Erika, grabbed her blue diamond necklace, and ripped it from her neck, before sprinting off into the darkness.

Everything had happened within a few seconds. I was struggling to breathe.

I was trying to reach up to Erika who now bent towards me; still in shock and panicking at what we had just been a part of, screaming desperately for help.

I was so concerned for her safety that I'd not realised the extent of the pain until my adrenaline levels started to wear off. Her screams had alerted a few passers-by from the strip who had rushed to help.

Slowly my breathing relaxed, but the pain in my ribs was unbearable. A young blonde woman was first to the scene and helped me to my feet, guiding me towards the wooden bench. 'What happened?' she asked Erika, easing me into the chair.

'Two people attacked us; they kicked Mark and ripped off my necklace.'

'I've called the police,' the woman said. 'Are you hurt?'

Struggling for breath, I told them I felt like my ribs were broken.

Within moments, the sounds of police sirens approached our location, and I gazed at Erika blankly, still shaken and shocked.

'Are you okay?' she whispered to me as the police officers approached us. I nodded and gave her a wink, not wanting her to worry any more than she needed to.

A non-uniformed officer introduced himself as Bert and asked whether I wanted an ambulance. He seemed more interested in what the two attackers looked like, and I thought I detected a bit of a British accent.

'I was tying my shoelaces, I didn't see a thing,' I replied

Erika was able to give an accurate description of the one who grabbed her necklace. The guy who put his right boot into my side was wearing a hood, so other than explaining his attire, neither of us knew what he looked like.

Bert gave out our descriptions to the other officers and said they had more local police in the area who would start the search. He handed me his contact card as the ambulance approached, saying he would get my statement later, once I was at the hospital.

The X-ray revealed two fractured ribs, but no internal bleeding. The doctors informed me that the best thing I could do was rest with little or no movement for the next few weeks, as there was no operational procedure that they could perform and that my ribs would heal in time. I had bruising from my right shoulder down to the bottom of my ribcage, which seemed to get darker by the minute but probably looked a lot worse than it was.

Bert, our friendly police friend, had visited the hospital, and we'd both given our statements, explaining in detail what had happened. He would be in touch if anything developed and said he would have a member of his team close by to keep tabs on us, just in case.

Just in case what? I wondered. We were mugged, nothing more than that, surely. Erika called the manager at the Bellagio and told him what had happened and asked for a decent supply of ice when we got back to the hotel. He sent the hotel limousine to the hospital to collect us and said two members of the hotel security team would escort us back to the villa. We were honoured guests and he was disgusted at what had happened in his hometown.

Holding on to Erika, I limped from the hospital to the awaiting limo, where two burly security men were waiting by the car.

'Are you okay?' Erika kept asking, still upset and in a state of shock.

'I'm fine baby, don't worry about me. I'm just glad you're okay.'

'But the necklace,' she replied, wiping tears from her eyes. 'I can't believe they took my beautiful necklace.'

I wiped the moisture from her cheek, trying to reassure her she need not worry. 'It's only a necklace, don't worry. Things could be a lot worse. You weren't harmed and I can only be thankful for that. I don't know what I would have done if they'd hurt you. We are insured for the necklace and we can get you another one.'

The mugging certainly allowed us to sober up from the wine and champagne we'd consumed earlier, although the alcohol had slightly helped with the pain, and it had started to wear off.

The hospital had given me plenty of powerful painkillers and told me to rest for the next few weeks, no exercise or lifting, and I had to curtail the alcohol. 'You will need to do all the work in bed tonight, babe. I'm on doctor's orders.'

She managed a smile as the limo pulled up to our villa and the driver helped me out.

28

Debrief

'This is a pretty unique situation, but it's one we need to use to our advantage.'

The MI6 team were back at the Las Vegas Intelligence Office for a debriefing, whilst an officer was stationed outside of the Bellagio Villa.

Simmons was standing as he always did when he gave one of his 'I've got a plan' speeches. 'We can get closer without them getting suspicious. Not too close, as we cannot deter the tags, but close enough to react a lot faster than last night.'

'Why the hell would the Tycoon's tags just take a necklace? It makes no sense.' Bissett asked.

Minto was disappointed at herself for allowing the robbery to take place, but slightly enlightened at the fact that it was only a necklace that went missing. 'They were quick, very quick. Their only agenda was the necklace. They had no interest in Davidson or the girl.'

'Do we have anything on the two tags?' Simmons asked, pacing the room.

Bissett placed two files onto the large oval desk. 'Sub A and Sub B, sir. The odd thing is that they have no association with the Tycoon. Petty thieves, both with criminal records, mostly robberies. No known associates and no known addresses. Sub B has a warrant out for unpaid fines, but other than that, nothing that stands out.'

'So, you're telling me this was a simple robbery and nothing more? Wrong place, wrong time? Are you joking me?' Simmons slammed his coffee cup onto the desk. 'We could have been compromised and two lowlife Vegas thieves are to blame?'

'Looks that way, sir,' replied Bissett.

'Nothing's coincidence in our world. You know that by now. Without question, this will be connected in some way. Get back out there for Christ's sake and be ready. This is the start of it. They're testing the ground. We cannot let this son of a bitch slip through our fingers again.'

29

A walk to destiny

'Our table is booked for 7 p.m., as long as you're sure you are gonna be okay.'

'I need to breathe some fresh air. If I don't get out of here soon, I'm gonna go mad.' It had been three full days since our visit to the hospital and I'd spent almost all of that time in bed. Erika had been amazing, running around after me without a single complaint. She was even on hand to help me in the bath, which I secretly rather enjoyed. A little too much enjoyment on the second day. I'd ordered her to get in with me and as we made love in the warm bubbles, I'd knocked my ribs on the side of the bath and almost passed out with the pain.

The hotel manager had arranged for our dinner to be cooked at the Picasso restaurant and then delivered to us.

Other than a little heavy breathing and obvious pain, I was physically fine and told Erika I didn't want to waste our holiday locked inside the villa. Las Vegas had more to offer than *MTV Cribs* and *CSI Miami,* and we couldn't hide away any longer.

We arrived at Caesars Palace just before seven, where we were directed to the Spa Tower. The French Restaurant, Guy Savoy, with its white walls and wooden trellis, was unassuming and elegant. The manager greeted us as we entered and welcomed us with a complimentary glass of champagne.

One glass won't hurt. I was looking forward to some champagne after three days of caffeine, painkillers and water. We sat at the chef's centre table, which had the added benefit of the executive chef and restaurant owner, Guy Savoy himself, cooking especially for us.

The first glass of champagne hit the spot, and I thought to hell with it, so ordered a bottle of Dom Perignon and we perused the menu for the evening's feast. We had not spent a single dime in the last three days, so tonight we would push the boat out.

For the first time since that night, Erika spoke about the robbery. 'I wonder if the muggers had been following us.'

'I don't know, maybe they just spotted us in the casino, eyed-up the necklace around your neck and followed us to the alleyway and took a chance?'

'Why us? There were hundreds of people on the casino floor. What makes us so special?'

'A blue diamond, perhaps? Or maybe we were just in the wrong place at the wrong time. We did win a lot of money that night.'

'That was the nicest present I've ever had, Mark. I can't believe those bastards stole it.'

I had nothing to say.

She smiled at me and changed the subject to lighten the mood slightly. 'I think I'm going to have the chicken. How about you?'

After a relaxing evening and one of the most spectacular meals we had ever consumed, we arrived back at the villa at around 2 a.m. and called our parents to check how things were going at home. Rather than worry everyone about the robbery, we had agreed to keep the incident to ourselves and tell them everything when we got back.

My mum and dad were in fine spirits, stuck at home due to the severe weather that was still causing chaos in the UK. The snow hadn't stopped for the last three days straight. 'We don't mind,' my mum said. 'It's quite nice spending time at home.'

My brothers Chris and Andy gave their usual tales of how much beer they'd consumed and asked more than once if Erika had actually woken up and realised the mistake she'd made.

Erika spoke with her parents, telling them she was having a great time and that we were getting on fantastically well. They asked about the hotel and she promised to email some photographs after the call.

It felt bad keeping them in the dark, but they would only worry. We finished the calls and curled up in bed to watch TV and no sooner had my head hit the pillow that I drifted off to a deep sleep.

I woke up in complete darkness, hearing a faint noise coming from the bathroom. I reached over to my left to find Erika was missing. As I turned around in bed to get comfortable, I heard her coughing and spluttering in the bathroom. I immediately panicked and jumped out of bed before creasing over in a ball with the shooting pains from my ribs.

'Shit,' I screeched, forgetting that my injury was still alive and kicking. I opened the bathroom door, to find her kneeling down over the toilet holding her stomach, her back and hair soaked with sweat.

'Oh my God, are you okay?' I asked.

'Yeah,' she managed to say softly. 'Migraine. They usually come without warning… '

I dipped a towel into some water and passed it to her to wipe her face.

'I'm sorry,' she said.

'Don't be silly, you don't need to be sorry at all. What can I do?'

'Not much. I have to sit it out. Please go back to bed.'

I woke up just before 7 a.m. Erika was sleeping. Gently, as not to disturb her, I crawled out of bed and walked to the kitchen area, made myself a coffee and sat at the breakfast bar, downing a couple of painkillers.

As I sipped my coffee, Erika appeared from the bedroom in one of the large, white Bellagio dressing gowns, looking rather glum and pale faced. She attempted a smile, sat on the chair next to me and dropped her head on my good shoulder.

'How are you feeling?' I asked, stroking her hair.

'Better,' she replied without moving.

'You can't fool me,' I replied, slowly lifting her head, staring into her eyes, which were red and tired looking. Her face was pale, and she had a high temperature. 'I'll nip out to the chemist for painkillers … I don't want to give you mine. Might be too strong?'

She nodded. 'Safer.'

Why don't you stay in bed today and I'll look after you for a change.'

'Thanks ... I just need to wait it out ...'

I marched her back to bed, leaving a large glass of water and a few headache tablets from the first aid kit. 'Go back to sleep and I will be back soon. Keep your phone by the bedside and if you need me, just call. I won't be long.' I kissed her head and left her in the darkness, showering in the opposite part of the villa. Although I felt awful leaving Erika in bed alone, she needed to sleep and it was going to work out well for me. I called James - my American work friend - and asked him if he was free to meet up at short notice.

'I can be in the hotel in half an hour,' he had said.

'Perfect.'

Walking out onto the Las Vegas strip, I felt a sudden coldness and became instantly wary of my surroundings. This was the first time since the robbery that I'd stepped outside onto the strip without Erika and without the hotel security close by. It was still early in the morning, but Vegas never sleeps and there were hundreds of people out. After ten minutes, I'd reached the 24-hour pharmacy, bought what I needed and headed back to the hotel.

30

A Potential Investment

For a successful businessman, James was still fairly young. At 29, he was the co-owner of a large electronics business in Los Angeles. His brother was his business partner. The two of them had built up the business from nothing and, as far as I was aware, they had a pretty solid company with dealings all over the US and Europe.

'What's with the bag?' asked James as we took a seat in the cafeteria next to the casino.

'I have a sick girlfriend and she's in bed,' I replied, holding up the bag of medication from the chemist.

'Girlfriend? That's a new one. I thought you were single.'

'Yeah, long story.' A waitress approached us and we ordered some coffee. As James and I reminisced about our amazing nights out in Los Angeles the conversation eventually turned to his 'situation'. For six months, I'd taken the lead on a new development for their business, and with hard work, long hours and mostly down to the relationship I had built with James, we had secured a new software package that would save their business 30% over the next three years. During a six-month period, I'd visited James several times to negotiate the contract. We'd hit it off immediately, being quite close in age and having similar interests. James had lived in Los Angeles his whole life and had driven the five hours to Vegas to not only meet me, but to take in a business meeting the previous day.

He told me the meeting had not been a success. It was with a potential investor who 'didn't have any balls.' 'It was about the chip I spoke to you about, remember?'

I nodded.

'It has huge potential and, until two days ago, I was in no rush to move things along. Anyway, circumstances have changed somewhat, and I came here to meet this so-called big-time investor, and to be honest, he was more interested in talking about himself and his achievements than actually listening to what I had to offer.'

'You were selling him the chip?' I asked naively.

'You really want me to bore you with the full details?' He took a sip of his coffee.

'Sure, why not.'

'Well, as you already know, just over ten years ago now, my brother and I started the business, developing processing chips for cell phones. Harry had taken a large redundancy from his previous employer and we used that money to pay our salaries, develop and test the chips, and then eventually travelled around the globe to find potential buyers. Following bad advice from a really shitty lawyer,' he continued, 'we sold the new chip we'd developed and all the rights to a large cell phone business in China for a million US dollars. At the time, it was our greatest achievement, and we used this money to invest back into the business for other developments and bigger ideas we had. Fast forward to a few years ago when we'd begun to substantially grow the company, then eventually we brought in a local law firm to look after our day-to-day legals. They nearly flipped when we told them about the chip and no matter how hard they tried, they couldn't pull back the rights from China. That ship had sailed and the scum bag lawyer had sewn up everything very nicely for the other side and left us without a loophole. The main reason they were so annoyed was that our chip has since become a major breakthrough in cell phone technology, for reasons I won't bore you with. Let's just say we should now be multi-millionaires if we'd not sold the full rights for such a low fee.'

'Wow, it must have been a major piece of work.' I was suitably impressed.

'Believe me, it was, but I guarantee it's nothing like the chip I've been developing for the past three years. You see, my brother was the money in the beginning as well as the salesman, and I was always the brains. We made a decent team. The chips were all my ideas, my developments, and then he would make contact with the relevant companies and negotiate the deals.'

I took a sip of my coffee, leaning forward slightly on my chair, hoping that this story had a decent ending.

'A few months ago, I finally finished development of our new chip, a major advance in GPS and tracking technology and after intense testing, securing patents, it is now ready to be offered to the market.'

'So where's the problem?'

'Well, two weeks ago, my brother and I had a huge fall out, and I mean huge. I was fed up with his lack of contribution to our already volatile relationship. He is lazy, has started to drink more, and was spending our business funds on luxury trips, which I now know were never about finding investors. I was just so busy with the development of the new chip that I guess I buried my head in the sand and allowed him to get on with his life, not thinking of the consequences.'

'Your own brother?'

'Yeah, tell me about it. We had a huge bust-up, and I told him exactly what I thought of him and he blamed me for losing out on our fortune a few years previous. He stormed out of the building and I've not seen or heard from him since. That was, until a week ago, when I walked into work to find a complete disaster.'

'What do you mean?'

'Well, he'd paid a little visit to our building in the middle of the night and completely destroyed everything in our labs. The machinery, components, spare parts, computers, paperwork, everything. That is, almost everything.'

'Almost?'

'Almost,' he said. 'When we were clearing up the mess, I noticed that the new chip, its components, all of the paperwork and computer equipment used to develop it had vanished. He'd stolen the chip and all the production information that goes with it and now he's disappeared. I've tried to call him, text him and email him. I've visited his home, but he has vanished. Then, two days ago, one of my work acquaintances called me and informed me he'd found some information that I may find useful.'

'Go on.'

'Well, my brother had offered my bloody chip, the one I developed, to a huge GPS business, and they are currently in negotiations. I have no doubt he is negotiating himself a rather comfortable payment.'

'But surely you have a copyright on the chip or signed contracts or something that won't allow him to do this without your signature?'

'He's my brother, Mark. I trusted him and we both technically own the rights to what the company produces. He created a contract clause that allowed either party to make and agree contracts.'

'Holy shit!'

James held up a finger and waved it in front of my face. 'But … I am not as stupid as he clearly thinks I am. After all, I invented the chip and I have copies of everything he destroyed. The problem I do have, however, is that he stole the actual prototype chip itself, the testing equipment, all the components, and the computers I used to develop it.' He took a deep breath, smiled, and continued. 'So I acted fast, I spent a lot of time and developed it considerably, I've patented it even further in terms of how it can be used and I've drilled it down to a specific industry and given it every kind of copyright I could find. I have also put our business into administration and started a new one in my name. In real terms, it's a variation of the old chip but a lot more advanced now. If my brother ever sees the new chip, he won't even recognise it.'

'There's a "but", isn't there?

'Yes,' he nodded. 'The bloody investor, the guy I met with this morning. I was hoping to go over my plans and ask him to invest money in my new company, in exchange for a percentage share in the new business which I've started. The money would have allowed me to mass-produce the chips, ready for our first order. I have three companies pushing me for mass trial, but I don't have the money to do it.'

He looked up and looked me straight in the eye. 'This should have been it, Mark. The big one.'

The bartender came over with a tray full of champagne glasses filled with tasty bubbles which we gladly accepted. The first cold sip was a delight.

James almost drained his glass before he spoke. 'This fucking investor was my last roll of the dice. When I eventually told him about my plans, he said it was not the sort of thing he was looking for. The prick could have just told me that on the telephone and saved me from wasting my time for absolutely no reason.'

'And you've no more investors lined up?'

He shook his head.

'How much were you looking for from your investor?'

'Well, I had offered him a 49% stake in the business for an investment of five million dollars'

I whistled.

'I know,' he said, 'it's a lot of money but I'd need that much to develop the prototypes and set up an operation for bulk production. As soon as the initial orders were under way, I would have floated the business on the stock exchange. His 49% share would have increased substantially, I mean huge, like tenfold, maybe more. I'm confident in the chip and its ability and I've no doubt it would have been a success, but thanks to that asswipe I've simply run out of time.'

It was about a minute before I spoke. James drained another glass of champagne.
'So, no doubt you came prepared, with documents and contracts.'

'Everything was ready for him and his sleazy lawyer to take away, read through and then sign, but they never really gave me a chance.'

'The chips, what exactly do they do and what are they used for?'

'It's all in the documents.'

'Tell me in a nutshell.'

'This is confidential, Mark. Okay?'

'My word is my bond.'

His voice lowered to almost a whisper. 'The chip can be installed in a golf ball. I know you like your golf, so this will be right up your street. Tell me, how many golf balls would you say you used in one round of golf?'

He was leaning forward now, clearly excited at his sales pitch.

'I'm not the best golfer the world has ever seen and there are way too many trees at my local course, so maybe six or seven?'

'Six or seven golf balls on every round,' he replied then gave a small whistle, obviously unimpressed. 'How many times a week do you play?'

'Twice.'

'Let's say a dozen balls a week then.'

'That's about right.'

'So about 600 balls a year.'

'Wow, yes, not to mention the stroke penalty on every lost ball.'

'Exactly. Now, imagine if I could show you a way where you'd never ever lose a ball again.'

'I'm all ears.'

'My microchip can be installed inside a golf ball. It uses a GPS tracking signal and reports to an electronic GPS scorecard that you can attach to your golf cart. When you cannot find the ball, the chip goes to work. Each scorecard can download to every single golf course in the world. You input the information prior to tee-off and the GPS will do the rest. So, when the ball is lost, you simply click the lost ball button on the scorecard and the GPS will direct you to your ball. It's as simple and as easy as that. It's been tested, it's a zero percent failure rate. Zero.'

Now I was seriously interested.

'A Titleist Pro V ball is around five dollars a ball, so crap golfers like you can save around three thousand a year if you use my little chip.' With a huge grin on his face, he sat back in his chair and continued. 'The chip conforms to golfing regulations and weighs practically nothing, so it does not affect the flight of the ball. It's copyrighted to hell and if I can get these mass-produced and then hit all the major manufacturers … can you imagine the potential?'

I sat upright, excited at the chip's possibilities and this huge untapped market. I'd read somewhere that over 60 million people play golf worldwide. What an opportunity. 'If these chips are as good as you say they are, then give me the legal documentation you were going to give your investor, the contracts, the full specifications, how they are produced and your sales projections.'

'You, Mark?'

'Yes. I'll get my legal team to take a look at them.'

He flopped back in his seat and let out a long sigh. 'It's a five million dollar investment, buddy. Surely you don't have that type of money to spare?'

I ignored his question. 'If you can give me all the documentation, I promise to get back to you in 24 hours with a yes or no.'

He was caught like a rabbit in the headlights. 'You have that sort of money, buddy?'

I nodded my head just once.

It sparked life back into James, who jumped up and told me to wait five minutes while he dashed to his room to fetch all the relevant documents.

I tried to think rationally. There was no harm in taking the documentation and telling him to give me a day to consider it. I had an idea and the perfect person who could review the figures and documents and then give me some honest advice.

James came bouncing back into the casino, holding two black briefcases.

'This is everything you will need,' he said, panting slightly, and placed both briefcases down on the ground next to me. He told me to read through the documents, hand them to my legal team and accountants and let him know by tomorrow if it was possible. He was heading back to LA in the afternoon and told me to call him once I'd made a decision.

'I'll do my best,' I said, playing it as cool as I could.

'You're my only hope, Mark. We need to act now before my brother tries to get out of the blocks first. Can you imagine the possibilities, especially if we can get the company floated or even sold to the highest bidder?'

'I'll be in touch as soon as I can, mate.'

I picked up the two briefcases and headed back to the villa.

31

Legal and Financial

I stepped back quietly into the villa, glancing at the clock in the hallway. I'd been away for just under two hours. I opened the bedroom door slightly, peeked my head in to see that Erika was asleep.

I headed to the large dining area, setting the two briefcases onto the table, and clicked them both open, revealing two piles of documents. I emptied the first case onto the table and started from the top. The first pack was a legal contract, for the transfer of a full 49% stake in the new company named, 'Twenty-Five Degrees Los Angeles'.

I scanned the document, which was full of legal terminology and from what I could gather, would indeed transfer the agreed stake to a yet unnamed third party.

The second, and largest document was a detailed contract of the microchip and its capabilities, and extensive schedules regarding the actual manufacture, including diagrams and pages upon pages of technical data. I left this one out to read in more detail later.

Opening the second case, I found that the top document was an audit report and documented business plan, which would be required if carrying out a sale or floatation and to also seek further investment. The report was complete and signed by independent auditors.

The final report showed the full financials of the business, including projected profit-and-loss reports, debtor reports, cost analyses, sale forecasts and more. As this was a new business, everything was a projected amount, but he'd attached the previous company's details along with it.

I was glad to see that James and the business looked to be prepared and ready for progression and that I had an awful lot of work to do if I really wished to become involved. I'd always wanted to have my own business, and this was starting to look like an offer simply too good to refuse, regardless of the financial risk.

I checked my watch and calculated the time difference in the UK. It was still the very early hours of the morning back home. Taking the large file I'd kept aside, I walked to the lounge and while Erika slept, I read the file from front to back, only stopping to down a few painkillers.

As I got up to take another painkiller, it happened. A sudden bolt of pain knifed me at the back of my skull. I fell to the floor and blacked out. When I came to, it took a couple of seconds to recognise where I was. I slowly sat up and then got up. I felt okay. Could this be a form of migraine? I had to get to a doctor as soon as I got home. I should have done so ages ago.

It was after lunch when Erika sauntered into the lounge, wrapped up in the large, white dressing gown. She looked rather pale and greeted me with a slightly forced smile. 'Morning,' she croaked.

'Good afternoon.' I kissed the top of her head as she cuddled into me on the sofa.

'What are you reading?' she asked.

'It's a bit of a long story. Let me put the kettle on and I will tell you all about it. Oh, and I went out to the chemist for you.' I handed her the bag of goodies.

For the next half hour, we sat together as I explained the morning's events, giving her all the details and showing her the contracts and legal paperwork.

'Five million dollars?' she said more than once.

'From what he's told me and from what I can see and have read so far, I think James is a genius and these microchips could actually be one of the best inventions I've ever seen. I know you're not feeling too good, but are you up for a bit of legal reading?'

'Yeah sure,' she replied with a sigh. 'I was hoping we could have a day just at the villa today, so this can keep me occupied for the day.'

Erika would be able to make sense of the legal documents and, in a few hours, I could make a call to the UK and have the accountancy paperwork checked over.

'Happy Christmas, Si. Did Santa Claus give you any nice gifts?'

It was 9 a.m. in the UK and if anyone would be up and about this early, then it would be Si.

'You know, the usual. Underwear and a blow-up sheep, what you doing calling me at this time of the morning and where the hell are you?'

He sounded groggy and tired, and after apologising for the early hour I got straight to business. 'I need your help. I'm considering going into a venture with a partner and before I say yes, I'd like you to check over some figures for me. I promise it will be worth your while.'

'Sure buddy, what figures are they?'

'It's a long story and I promise to tell you all about it later, but time is of the essence. I need to get this checked out as soon as possible, Si. I can get it scanned and emailed over to you now. Will you call me as soon as you read it?'

'Sure, email it over to me now, mate.'

'Thanks, Si. I knew I could count on you.'

The receptionist was a great help and within ten minutes all of the documents were scanned and emailed with a note reminding Si to call me as soon as he'd finished. He would start reading as soon as it arrived, so I guessed I would hear from him later that afternoon. Hopefully, he would confirm that everything looked okay and the offer of 49% share in the business was indeed as valid as it sounded and, more importantly, worth the investment.

Erika had taken her tablets, and we lazed around the villa and around the pool, reading the documentation and chatting.

We had decided to keep off the booze for a few days and ordered a healthy lunch, some freshly squeezed juice and lots and lots of ice water.

'What a sorry sight,' I said, glancing up and down at the two of us as we lay by the side of the pool. 'My broken ribs, you vomiting everywhere. This was meant to be a fun filled trip to Vegas and here we are, both falling to pieces.'

'I know,' she laughed. 'And now we are working, who's idea was that?'

'I certainly know how to show a lady a good time don't I? I'll make it up to you though, I promise.'

'Most of this is pretty standard,' she said, changing the subject. 'It all looks professional and legally everything is in place. You would be part owner of the business, a director and entitled to a share of the profits that come with it or from a sale or floatation, so from a legal point of view I guess it's a goer. What about the product, are you sure it's worth such a big investment?'

'It all looks good to me. If he can manage to mass produce the chip and sell to the highest bidder, I think we could have just hit a gold mine.' Just as I was finishing my sentence, the phone rang,

It was Si. 'So, I've read through it all and financially everything is in order. But I do have one question.'

'What is it?'

'Where the hell are you going to get five million dollars?'

His question lingered for a moment, and I tried to skirt by the issue as best as possible. 'That's another long story, Si. I don't have the time just now to explain. Let's just say my trip to Vegas has been extremely profitable and I have a chance to use it wisely. Erika and I have checked all the legal paperwork and the specifications of the chips. Now we just need confirmation that the figures look correct and that will be the last piece of the jigsaw as it were.'

'Then I guess you just bought yourself a business,' he said. 'You're not in any trouble out there, are you?'

'Trouble? No way, we're having a ball,' I said, looking at Erika, who raised an eyebrow.

'Okay, Mark. Well, you just be careful.'

'Don't worry, everything is great out here and I promise when we get home, I will thank you properly for this.'

'You don't need to do that. Enjoy the rest of your trip and let me know if you need anything else.'

'Thanks, Si. And keep this between us for the moment?'

'I will.'

32

Room 310

'His name is James Woods. He's an electronics manufacturer out of Los Angeles. Landed two days ago in Vegas and is staying at the Bellagio Hotel.'

Simmons threw a small brown file onto the desk while he updated the agents on a conference line. 'He met with John Helmsley within hours of arriving here, a big-time investor with big time finances. Four hundred million pounds at the last count, so no doubt the meeting was about investment into his business.'

'Davidson has only had the money a week, and he's meeting with investors already?' Bissett asked.

'Looks like it was two separate meetings, completely non-related. Davidson and Woods are work acquaintances from the past and it looks like Woods' investor didn't want to take up his offer.'

Simmons was pacing the floor with his third espresso of the day.

'And Davidson is investing? What's our line on Woods? Is he involved with the Tycoon?' Minto asked.

'At this stage we don't know, Woods is en route back to LA, so our team will stick a tail on him when he lands. What's our status on the happy couple? Is there any movement?'

Minto was holed up in Room 310 of the Bellagio, which gave a direct line view - using telescopic binoculars - into the rear garden of Davidson's villa, where they spent most of their time sunbathing.

'Nothing much,' she said. 'But Davidson came back with two hefty briefcases and they've been reading documents for hours.'

'Woods handed them over in the casino,' Bissett replied. 'I guess it relates to the required investment.'

'It is,' Minto said, 'he was on the phone to an accountant in the UK earlier and sent him a rake of figures to check over. I don't think this has anything to do with the Tycoon, I think it's a genuine friend-to-friend investment, nothing more.'

'Okay. See how it pans out,' Simmons said, 'and take nothing for granted. At least five of the Tycoon's regular tags have arrived in Vegas and his Number Two is already here. If it's going to happen, then it's going to be soon. Don't take your eyes off them and report back later.'

The phone lines disconnected.

33

Head over Heels

In a matter of hours, we had agreed the contracts, signed legal documentation and I had actioned the transfer of funds to the corporate bank of Los Angeles.

I guess in business you need to take a risk and you need to spend money to make money. Although I was fully behind the deal, I also knew that if everything failed, I would have said goodbye to five million dollars, but I still had a substantial pot to fall back on. I also wanted to back James and give his business a chance. Furthermore, if it went as well as expected, then I could make a serious profit and be part of a reputable business in Los Angeles.

After we'd discussed it all again, Erika had fallen asleep early, saying that her migraine was lifting. It was at that point I decide to make a few surprises to make up for staying indoors for the past few days.

I sent a rather long email to Bob, telling him that Erika was unwell, and gave him an overview of the robbery. I wanted to make it up to Erika, and Bob was only too keen to assist me in my plans, informing me he would get to work immediately.

If Erika was feeling up to it, we would hit the strip the next morning and see more of the sights. For the day after, I needed Bob's help in arranging a rather special trip. I explained what I was looking for and asked him to let me know as soon as everything was arranged.

We showered, dressed and went for breakfast in the Café Bellagio. The restaurant was beautifully decorated with light, airy architecture and had arched windows, allowing superb views of the pool and garden. The setting was romantic and charming.

'I love this type of place,' Erika whispered as she gazed around the room. 'It looks so historic ... beautiful.' She was looking radiant again. Her migraine was over.

I squeezed her hand. 'Reminds me of Italy. Now there is a place seeped in history and beauty. I promise I will take you on our next trip. You will absolutely love it.'

'What are you going to do when we get back into the real world?' she asked as the waiter approached and placed a huge plate of fresh, hot pastries in front of us.

'I've had an idea about the money. I don't want to tell everyone that I won the lottery, that's for certain. The media are still circling like vultures to find the winner.'

'What's your idea then?'

'I'm going to tell my parents and my brothers about the win but everyone else, I was thinking of saying that we'd had a big win in Vegas, but nowhere near the amount of the lottery win.'

Erika finished her mouthful of croissant and thought about it for a moment.

'Actually, that could work, but how much are you going to say you won?'

'I'm not sure, maybe ten million dollars? That's still a life-changing amount of money, but enough to keep anyone off the scent of such a huge amount.'

'I still can't believe you won all that money, Mark.'

'I know. It still doesn't seem real to me.'

'Are you sure you want me to tag along with you?' she asked, looking a little sheepish.

Although we'd been together for a very short period, I knew in my heart that Erika was the one for me. I had wanted to be close to her since puberty and now that I was, I would do everything in my power to make her happy. 'I want you to be with me. I want to travel the world and grow old with you.' I leaned forward and placed my hand on hers. She smiled and sat forward as we kissed. Shivers still cascaded down my spine every time she was near me. 'I know we've only been together for a short time but it feels so right, like it was meant to be.'

'In that case,' she replied, 'I would be thrilled to have an adventure with you, Mr Davidson.' She leaned forward and kissed me again, gently on the lips.

The rest of our day was blissful and by far the best we had experienced in Las Vegas. When we left the restaurant, we had strolled up to the MGM Grand Hotel, further up the main strip. The Bellagio manager had reluctantly obeyed our orders and pulled back his security staff to allow us some privacy. I knew they would be in the background and I was okay with that, as long as they were out of sight.

The restaurant manager had recommended the spa facilities in the hotel and this fit with our agenda perfectly. A quick call had booked us an afternoon of spa luxury. I decided on an Indian head massage and hot towel shave, and Erika had chosen a manicure and pedicure and then a visit to the hair salon. The facilities were fantastic, the ultimate in relaxation. It was perfect and just what we both needed after what seemed like an eventful week. After hours of pampering and the most relaxing afternoon for as long as I can remember, we were driven to the exclusive Addiction restaurant for an early dinner.

Our last stop, watching the Tony winning, *Jersey Boys* was fantastic and our front row seats were worth every cent. Later I gave Erika my own rendition of *Can't take my eyes off you*.

.

34

Pilot in situ

'It's happening. This is going to be our shot, people.'

Simmons had called the entire team to the briefing room. Diagrams filled the huge whiteboard. For the last two hours they had gone through a detailed plan of action.

'We've managed to replace the chopper pilot with one of our own, who will track their movements and we'll follow them to their destination. If it's going to happen, then it will happen once they land. Bissett, Minto, I want you both in the chopper following. Dave, Nick, I want you to have three teams surrounding the landing area.'

Walking over to the whiteboard, Simmons pointed at the diagrams, going over it again. 'There are three caves here, here and here. Stay concealed and alert. This is where the pickup has to take place and the tags have already moved trucks into the cave here,' he said, pointing. 'This is our one and only shot before extraction.'

35

Tension in the air

It was 6 a.m. the next morning when I woke and gently lifted myself out of bed, careful not to wake Erika. She looked so peaceful that I could not help but smile as I left the bedroom.

I made coffee and checked my emails. Bob had replied to my request. All of the arrangements had been made and he'd even listed a small itinerary, together with contact numbers, should I need to speak to anyone. 'Good old Bob,' I whispered under my breath.

'A surprise?' Erika asked as I walked into the bedroom, dripping wet from the shower I just took and sat on the edge of the bed. 'What kind of surprise?'

'I can't tell you too much, can I? Or it wouldn't be a surprise. All I will say is I promise it will be a day you will never forget.'

'Give me at least a hint, then.' she replied as she climbed onto my lap.

'Don't flutter your eyelids at me,' I said, smiling. 'You will need to wait and see. Now get your sexy ass in the shower and I'll order us some breakfast.'

A pillow hit the back of my head as I walked out of the bedroom and I heard Erika giggle as she ran into the bathroom before I could retaliate.

'So where are we going?' she asked, as she pulled herself closer to me in the cool leather seat of the limo.

'We're off to the airport'

'The airport?'

'Yep.'

The limo eased through the airport and headed to a private hanger, north of the main terminal building. Erika was glancing out of the window from left to right, trying to make sense of where we were going

'A helicopter?' she asked as the limo slowed to a snail's pace in front of one of the large, shiny choppers.

'You guessed it,' I said. 'I've never been on one of these, have you?'

'Never,' she replied, holding her hand over her mouth. 'I'm scared.'

'Don't be scared. They are just as safe as a plane. We'll be fine.'

The limo stopped, settled at the rear of the helicopter, and the driver opened our door. There was a cool breeze and a slight chill in the air as Erika linked my arm and we approached our welcoming committee.

We were greeted by the pilot, Captain Harrison and his co-pilot, First Officer Hardy, who was freakishly tall and muscular, and invited us to walk through the hangar into a waiting area.

For the next twenty minutes, we sat through a rather boring safety briefing. I could feel a slight tension from the way Erika was holding my hand when they displayed the lifejackets, and I had to admit I felt slight anxiety myself.

The captain explained the plans for our trip, which lightened Erika's mood somewhat. We would take off in approximately thirty minutes and fly for just under an hour, taking in views of the Hoover Dam, Lake Mead and, of course, the Grand Canyon.

Once in the canyon, we would settle on the banks of the Colorado River, where a champagne lunch would await us. We could then stroll up the river and enjoy the views before our own private river rapids ride down the Colorado River.

Afterwards, the helicopter would wait to take us back around the canyon and fly directly to the Luxor

Hotel on the Vegas strip, where dinner reservations were made at the Tender restaurant.

'Oh my God,' Erika said, 'how on earth did you arrange all of this without me knowing?'

'I have my ways.'

'It sounds amazing,' she said as the captain excused himself to carry out final checks on the chopper.

A waitress entered and left a large tray with tea, coffee, water and a variety of breakfast pastries and fresh fruit.

'I don't know if I can eat anything. My stomach is in knots,' Erika announced.

I was starving and grabbed a piping hot, crispy croissant. I looked outside at the hangar. There was a private jet parked up at the rear and another black helicopter in the centre. There were a few men in overalls engaged in some sort of repair work to the engine.

'Mark, Erika, the helicopter is ready for you if you would care to follow me.'

My stomach immediately tightened as a uniformed lady escorted us towards the chopper and the hefty first officer ushered us onboard the aircraft. We were handed a headset each.

The seating area was huge, enough for another six people and as there were only two of us, we would at least enjoy the comfort and plenty of space. We were told to buckle up and put on our headphones as the pilot started the rotors and my stomach was churning with nerves as the noise levels increased.

'Are you okay?' I asked Erika.

'No, I need a drink!'

The captain gave us a thumbs-up, and the chopper shuddered. A few seconds later, it lifted gently into the air.

Erika had tightly linked my legs with her feet and her hands were gripping the rail at the side of her.

'Don't worry,' I said. 'There's a parachute under your seat.'

I received a slap on my leg for my ill attempt at humour. I looked out of the window and noticed that the other helicopter's rotors had started.

I was surprised at the smoothness of the ride and even Erika managed a nervous grin as we flew towards the strip. The views were spectacular and the magnitude of the hotels was unbelievable. 'There's the Bellagio,' I said, pointing down towards our hotel, just as the large water display was in full flow.

The chopper circled the strip, taking in the impressive views and then built altitude before heading out towards the rocky desert.

'Sit back and enjoy the ride,' the captain said through our earphones. 'Next stop is the Grand Canyon.'

It was a good twenty minutes into the flight when the captain announced we were on approach towards our first landing point. The views were even better than I imagined and as far as the eye could see, were rocky red mountains and long, narrow drifting streams. Mother Nature was presenting herself in the most dramatic fashion, and I sat back in awe of her beauty.

As Erika and I stared out of the right-hand window, I noticed out of the corner of my left eye that the first officer had reached down at his feet and was rummaging in his flight bag for something.

I looked in horror as he appeared to pull out a small handgun and a thousand thoughts bounced around my head. I had enough military background to know that the handgun also had a silencer attached to the end. What the fuck was he up to? In a scene reminiscent of a Hollywood movie, he raised the gun towards the captain's head and squeezed off two shots. We were wearing headsets; we didn't hear a thing, but the sudden pull back action from the gun gave no doubt that he had just fired the weapon and the captain's skull jerked back violently, sending blood, brains and skull bone onto the door.

Erika screamed out loud as the captain's body slumped forwards, only held in place by his seat belt. The gunman steadied the controls and turned, looked at us without saying a word, and pointed his gun directly at us. The fear hit me unlike anything I had ever felt in my life, and I froze. I'd tried to remember my training from so long ago and took a deep breath. I had to keep calm, take stock of the situation, and think rationally.

Erika's hand gripped me tightly as the co-pilot switched on the microphone and began to speak.

'Mr Davidson,' he said. His accent was eastern European. 'Do exactly what I say and you and girlfriend will be safe. Try to be clever boy, I kill her and feed her to my dog. Understand?'

I nodded and unexpectedly felt a warm sensation in the seat. Erika's bladder had failed her, and she was locked in shock as I looked at her, tears streaming down her face.

I needed to stay calm, remove the emotion. 'What do you want?' I managed to say.

'No questions, Mr Davidson, do you hear?'

I nodded in response.

'Sit in seat and do not move or speak. If you do, you will both die before we touch ground.' He turned around in the seat facing forward and turned the chopper sharply to the left, immediately decreasing altitude. He leaned over the captain's body and released the seatbelt as the corpse fell limply onto the door.

As he slid over to the captain's side of the cockpit, he released a catch on the door and it swung open as a blast of cold air filled the cabin. With a firm kick the dead body tumbled out into the abyss.

Erika screamed again and grabbed me tightly. The co-pilot relocked the captain's door and clicked himself back into his seat, before swinging the chopper in a tight arc, 180 degrees.

Even during my time in the Marines, I could never have imagined anything like this. As we began to descend, I glanced outside as the helicopter approached a large clearing in the canyon.

Simmons watched the tracker from the control room. He couldn't quite fathom it. Why have they changed plans at this point? It makes no sense.

36

Separated

The chopper's pace decreased and as we approached the bottom of the canyon, I noticed two large, black 4x4 vehicles waiting.

'Fuck, holy fuck.' The words just left my mouth and Erika looked up at me, her eyes wide.

The gunman turned around, pointing his gun at my head. 'I said quiet,' he shouted, glaring at me before turning back in the seat to complete the descent.

It wasn't possible, was it? Surely not. We weren't being kidnapped, were we?

My brain went into overdrive. Initially, I thought the shooting was perhaps just a grudge, maybe an act of terror, mistaken identity or even a simple theft of a five million dollar chopper. But now, seeing the vehicle doors opening, I realised that there was a far more valuable cargo within easier reach.

The chopper hovered and found a clearing a small distance from the 4x4's. My heart was pounding and Erika was wiping tears from her eyes.

'I'm sorry,' I mouthed to her and as she embraced me, the engines started to slow the rotors of the chopper. I hugged her tightly. There was nothing else I could do.

The door of the chopper opened and two large men, dressed head to toe in light brown desert camouflage overalls, pointed their bulky machine guns at us. They motioned for us to exit the chopper.

The co-pilot opened his window and shouted something at them. Russian. Definitely Russian.

I had no idea what he had just said, but the first heavy approached us, grabbing Erika by the arm.

'With me,' he spat as he dragged her towards the front vehicle.

I reacted too hastily and shouted 'No!' as I lunged towards her and grabbed her arm. The second gunman punched me hard in the head and as I staggered backwards, rammed the barrel of his large machine gun with full force directly into my chest. I buckled backwards, the pain in my already tender ribs excruciating.

Erika cried out for help, but there was nothing I could do as she was dragged away from me.

She was already in the back of the first car, both rear doors now closed, as I was physically pushed towards the second car.

'In!' raged the gunman, motioning with his gun to the back seat of the second vehicle. I got into the car and moved to the middle seat. As I turned to look at him, he rammed the butt of his gun into my temple. The last thing I remember was a falling sensation and then complete darkness.

37

End of the Track

'Oh fuck sir, you're not going to believe this. It's the captain, the bloody captain.'

Bissett had been tracking at a discreet distance and had spotted the captain's body on the rocks of the canyon, the tracker still giving off its signal but the splattered body unrecognisable, only the uniform giving the game away.

'What do you mean?' Simmons snapped.

'It's the captain, sir, not the chopper. His body is in the canyon. There's blood everywhere sir. He's definitely dead by the looks of it.'

As they dropped to inspect the body, the black chopper they had been tracking came into view and veered away from them.

Bissett screamed, breathlessly, 'Follow it, follow the fucking thing!'

38

A Cell

It was a cold and wet sensation that rained down on my face that brought me round. As I opened my eyes slightly, another force of ice-cold water slammed into my face, taking my breath away as I tried to piece together what was going on.

I forced myself to sit upright. A tall, scruffy man hovered with an empty bucket. I tried to focus on him, but the room was poorly lit. He seemed satisfied that I was now fully awake and inched backwards out of a door at the back of the room. He slammed it shut, and I heard keys rattling.

My head throbbed, and I felt dizzy as I tried to get my bearings. The floor and walls were like ancient cobbles, the floor covered with wet straw.

I got up slowly, using the stone wall for balance. I took a few minutes controlling my breathing with deep, quick breaths and then consciously stretched in every direction before finally making circular movements with my head.

The ceiling of the room was quite low and without any effort, I was able to touch it as I reached up. The floor, walls and ceiling were all made of the same, dark grey and misshaped cobbles that were damp to the touch, no doubt due to the chilly temperature and a lack of light. The room measured approximately fifteen square feet and had nothing more than a stained mattress in the opposite corner.

The little light there was, was provided by a single candle.

I stumbled sluggishly towards the door, my right hand nursing the newly formed swelling on the front of my head. On inspection, the door was large, heavy duty and made of dark wood, maybe oak, with no windows or locks on the inside. There wasn't even a handle. I studied it for a few minutes, feeling my way around the top and bottom, revealing no holes or cracks anywhere. The only way to open the door would be from the outside.

I shuffled towards the mattress, clambered onto it, and lay down with my head in my hands. I curled up into the foetal position, my mind racing with thoughts of Erika and what was happening to her. I began to sob uncontrollably. I wanted nothing more than to fall asleep and never wake up.

I had no idea of the time I had been out cold, or indeed where the hell I was. The terror of the unknown began to punish my consciousness. As I lay with my thoughts and my tears, I closed my eyes and allowed my mind to drift.

It was a voice that brought me round this time.

'Stand up.'

A man dressed in desert camouflage was pointing a machine gun at my face, and I was suddenly thrust back to reality as I tried to remain calm.

'Stand up,' he repeated, standing back a step or two to give me room.

I struggled to my feet.

He backed away from me slowly. 'Follow.' He waved his gun towards the door. He backed up to the doorway and then stepped to the side of the room, allowing me to walk past him and through the entrance of the doorway.

My stomach tightened as I edged through the doorway and he poked me in the back with the weapon, guiding me up the dingy corridor to the left. It had the same damp stench of the small room I'd been held in. We progressed slowly up a pebble pathway, the walls identical to that of my cell. I gathered a little strength, told myself to stay alert and ready for any surprises. The corridor itself was as poorly lit as my prison cell, with small wall candles lighting the way and making it difficult to see for any distance.

The long pathway eventually ended and opened up into a vast space. My guard ordered me to stop and edged around my position, his gun pointing at my chest. He was at least a few inches taller than me, mid-forties, with a smooth shaved head and an unshaven, round face. There was another man, also with a machine gun. He looked angry. Is this the moment I'm going to die?

I started to plead for my life and didn't know why. 'Please, don't kill me. You have the wrong person, please, where is the girl? The girl, please …'

'Mr Davidson.' Another man had entered the room. 'You are not here to die, you are here to answer questions.'

A foreign accent, but well-spoken.

I turned to him. 'Who the hell are these people and what do they want from me?'

The first gunman grabbed my arm and dragged me towards the centre of the room. I tried to take a mental note of my surroundings. There was a large light hanging in the middle of the room that gave a small amount of illumination, but the outer walls were completely lost in the darkness.

The floor was flat, filled with gravel and stone, and as the gunman and I walked, it crunched and echoed around the room.

He stopped me directly under the light, where a white plastic chair had been placed in my honour. He slammed me into it. I winced as pain shot across my ribcage. 'Where is Erika? What have you done to her? Why are you doing this to me?'

'Your name is Mark Davidson, yes?'

The voice interrupted my train of thought. It was close and coming from directly behind me. As I turned, the voice screamed at me.

'Face front!'

'Yes, yes, okay.' Sweat was dripping from my forehead and my breathing was erratic. Stay calm, Mark, I told myself.

'Now. Answer question.'

'Yes, that's my name,' I replied.

'Date of birth is 23 August 1984.'

'Yes.'

'Your home is in Stella Road, Newcastle, UK, yes?'

'Yes.'

'Passport number MD1144235, yes?'

'I don't know my passport number.'

He let out a deep sigh. And then something was thrown over my head and landed a few feet in front of me.

'Pick,' he shouted, clearly annoyed at my lack of response at even the simplest of requests.

Calmly, I edged forwards and bent down to collect the item from the floor. My heart almost stopped as I felt a cold shudder run down my spine. It was my leather wallet that only 24 hours ago was securely locked away in the safe at the villa. Inside should be my credit cards and passport.

'Your passport number is MD1144235, yes?' His voice was stern as he exaggerated each letter, pausing for a second between each syllable.

I took out my passport and opened it. 'MD1144235, yes,' I replied. 'This is me.'

'Mr Davidson, on 19 December this year you won the world's biggest lottery jackpot, yes?'

And there it was. The one and only reason why I was now sitting in the middle of a cave, being interrogated by some Russian mafia gang lords or whoever the hell they were. They knew all about the money. These people knew exactly who I was, where I lived and how much money I had won. How could this have happened?

My brain went into overdrive, and my nervous system took full control of my body. I could feel the anger building up inside of me. What do I do? Lie? Do I just deny it? If I lie, would they kill me? They were clearly professional, what was the point in lying?

'Mr Davidson, answer the question.'

After three or four seconds, I felt the familiar nudge of the barrel of a machine gun to the rear of my skull. He held the position for a few seconds without saying a word and it was at that point my brain took a realistic control of the situation.

'Yes,' I said with a sigh, defeated. 'What do you want from me?'

He told me to stand, and I was on my feet immediately.

'No talk,' he said and pressed the gun into my back. He told me to walk, and I stumbled back to the entrance of the corridor as I continued to ask questions.

'No talk,' he repeated and stabbed me in the back to speed up my pace.

We arrived at the entrance to my cell and, pointing the gun at my chest, he unlocked the door. He pushed open the door and threw me inside. He closed and locked the door behind me.

I slammed the door with my fists and screamed at him. 'Please, where is the girl who was with me? Please!'

It was no use. There was nothing but silence on the other side of the door. The gunman had disappeared, and I was once again alone in the dark.

39

Alpha Team on The Way

'The chopper is down, I repeat, the chopper is down.' Bissett was screeching over the radio in a panic. 'Sir, permission to land and check it out.'

'Granted,' Simmons replied. 'What the hell is going on?'

'We're approaching, sir. I will switch on the live feed.'

The chopper approached and landed a few hundred meters from the wreckage. The black helicopter was fully ablaze, pumping masses of thick black smoke into the Vegas skyline.

'Can you see this?' asked Bissett, recording the wreckage and transmitting it back to the Las Vegas office. 'There are no bodies that I can see.'

'Of course there are no bodies, they have been kidnapped and the chopper was set alight. Sons of bitches must have known we were watching them.' Simmons was furious, cursing down the radio. 'Get in the fucking chopper and circle the area. Stay low and keep looking. Surely they can't be far. Alpha Team is on the way.'

40

A Familiar White Chair

It felt like I'd been alone for hours. I was tired and drained of energy. My body had been so tense for such a long time that it was now beginning to seize up. Although I was drifting in and out of sleep on the piss-stained, insect-infected mattress, I prayed to anyone who would listen that Erika was somewhere safe and unharmed, but my mind would simply not rest.

The question-and-answer session had allowed them to establish who I was, but more importantly, they knew that I'd won the lottery jackpot.

I was puzzled why they hadn't asked me for any other information. Were they going to demand money from me, perhaps even ransom me to the

World Lottery? After all, this scenario was the worst World Lottery could imagine. Nobody would play the lottery again.

Or were they just playing this out to scare me?

Where was Erika, and what did they want from her in all of this? I was filled with unanswered questions and felt completely helpless. I closed my eyes and tried to empty my mind, telling my body to relax. I focused on my breathing again and wondered where Erika was.

It felt like many hours had passed, when I heard the rattle of keys.

He stormed into my cell. 'Up!' he shouted.

I turned to get my bearings and faced yet another gun barrel pointing towards me. I jumped forward in a panic, holding onto the wall, and pulled myself to my feet. 'What? What the fuck do you want from me?'

I was starting to feel angry. I needed to get a grip on the situation and stop playing into their hands.

'Walk,' he demanded. He stood aside as I inched past him. He was stocky but compact, like a rugby player, and in the dimly lit room I could now see the scar on the top of his shaved head. It ran all the way to the bottom of his chin.

My military instincts were urging me to attack, to take him by surprise, but common sense told me to hold off until I knew Erika's whereabouts.

I steadied myself against the wall as I walked towards the end of the dark corridor and approached the interrogation area. The doors were open this time, filling the place with light and a welcome breeze from somewhere. I closed my eyes just for a second to feel the air as it hit my face.

The area was more like a cave and in the centre, where I had sat earlier, they had set up four desks, which were filled with computers and what looked like power generators.

In the right corner of the cave was a sand-coloured, camouflaged military vehicle and a gunman stood by the side with a machine gun around his neck. A second gunman patrolled by the door.

The thug who had collected me grunted and poked his gun in my back. 'Move.'

I inched towards the centre of the cave and he stopped me in front of the computers with a shout loud enough to wake the dead. 'HALT!'

The white plastic chair I'd sat in earlier was once again in front of me. The gunman grabbed me by the arm and shoved me into the seat. He stood to the right of me and a fourth gunman appeared from behind him, standing to my left. If they wanted to make me feel frightened or indeed intimidated, they were doing a fantastic job. I tried my utmost to look cool and relaxed. 'What do you want from me?' I asked, looking at the gunman to my left.

The gunman on my right walked over to the table and located a small black monitor. Without saying a word, he flicked a switch, and it sparked into life.

There, in front of me, was Erika. She sat on a mattress in a room which, was a replica of mine. I did not move. I tried to make sense of what I was seeing. My mind was racing, and it took every ounce of willpower I had not to jump from the chair and scream at the screen, at the gunmen, at anyone.

With extreme difficulty, I stared blankly at the monitor and told myself not to play their games, to keep quiet and to hide my emotions. It was obvious they were trying to get a reaction from me and rather than jump and cause a scene; I sat perfectly still.

'Mr Davidson.'

The familiar voice came from behind me, the lead gunman who had questioned me earlier.

'You can see, your girlfriend is safe. She is tired, hungry and confused, but otherwise fine. Mr Davidson, first, we need to have your full attention, yes?'

I finally snapped. 'Are you fucking stupid? You have my girlfriend locked in a dungeon, and you four crazy fucking people are standing over me with guns. How much more of my fucking attention do you want?'

For my outburst, one of the gunmen casually walked over and swung his right fist, connecting fully with my chin, which knocked me backwards onto the floor. The pain shot through my skull and the fall backwards knocked the wind out of me as I cracked my injured ribcage on the way down. I groaned in pain and held my jaw as the second gunman pulled my arm and yanked me to my feet. He dumped me back into the chair.

'Mr Davidson, please,' he whispered, 'it would be better if you keep mouth shut, yes?'

I was struggling to breathe, and all I could think of was Erika. Rather than replying, I merely nodded my head and thought it may be best to stay quiet for the time being, until they told me exactly what they wanted.

'Excellent. Now, Mr Davidson, we need you to do something and you are to follow exact instruction, yes?'

Again I nodded.

He handed me a small laptop computer, and a printed list of instructions as he walked round the desks to the main area, to where the other computer units were. 'Okay, you will now log into all of your email accounts,' he said, tapping the screen of his laptop. He waved the gun at me as if I needed to be reminded of what could be in store. I nodded.

'We need access to everything. We want all your passwords, your contacts, even your Facebook and Twitter account details, your followers and your friends.'

Within ten minutes and in complete silence I'd laid bare my life.

'Well done. Mr Davidson, it is best for you to cooperate. We have work to do now, so you may leave us.' He waved to one of the other heavies, who immediately marched over to my position and gave his usual one word order.

'Up.'

'Please,' I said, trying to stall, deciding to push my luck a little. 'I need food, water and I need to go to the toilet.'

He paused for a moment and then shouted something to the other heavy near the wooden doors. The door guard walked down towards the army vehicle and collected a package. As he walked back towards me, he threw the package in my direction. I leaped forward and managed to just catch it in my hands.

As we slowly trudged down the corridor again, I quickly unzipped my trousers and relieved myself, taking care not to alert my companion behind me. I finished just as we approached my cell.

He threw me into the room and locked the door behind me.

The package they'd given was a basic army food ration pack, which I laid out onto the mattress in front of me. Muesli, chili con carne, chocolate chip crème desert, flapjack, isotonic orange energy powdered drink, hot chocolate and a small bottle of water. Although I was not in the slightest bit hungry, I knew I had to eat to keep my strength up if I had any chance of getting out alive.

I slid down onto the floor and started to nibble on the flapjack. I began to get things straight in my mind.

Was Erika somewhere nearby in another cell? Her room looked identical to mine. Maybe she was close by. Was this just about the money or had we fallen into something a lot messier? And after the money, what then?

I think I knew the answer to that question. I hadn't been blindfolded. I could identify every single one of them. I closed my eyes and curled up on the mattress, chewing slowly on the flapjack, trying to relax my body and get some rest. Each question had an unhappy answer.

41

A Slim Silhouette

A shooting pain in the back of my head interrupted my deep sleep. The stabbing sharpness attacked the rear of my skull, making me wince in agony. I held my head with both hands and curled up tightly on the scruffy mattress.

The pain lasted for about a minute and then vanished. I slowly sat up on the mattress, rubbing the back of my head. On top of everything, I had a nagging concern that everything wasn't quite right with my health and I still hadn't visited a doctor.

I stood up. I was stiff as a board and I spent 15 minutes stretching, another 15 minutes jogging on the spot, and then I forced myself through 100 press-ups and 100 sit-ups. The endorphins kicked in and my head cleared a little. I felt a little better.

As I walked past the locked door, I was convinced I could hear a faint noise coming from outside, and it stopped me in my tracks. Quickly, I pressed myself hard against the door and pushed my right ear onto the small crack between it and the wall. Keeping perfectly still for a few moments, I close my eyes and listened.

I almost convinced myself that my mind was playing tricks and as I was about to give up, I heard it again. This time it was clear and, realising what it was, I jumped back from the door and started to kick and scream at the top of my voice.

'You bastards! No … no … what the fuck are you doing?' My throat felt like it was going to explode as I kicked and punched the door over and over again.

It was Erika; it was her screaming, without question. What were these cruel lunatics doing to her? I kicked the thick wooden door and screamed for at least five minutes, but my efforts fell on deaf ears.

Eventually, I stopped kicking and slumped back to the mattress, where I sat down in my usual spot. What did they want from Erika, and why was she screaming? They had all of my information. What could she tell them?

My emotions were shot to pieces, and I started sobbing. My whole world had been changed in a matter of hours and I'd gone from the happiest man on the planet to the most miserable. I grabbed the bottle of water and was just about to take a drink when the keys rattled into the lock and the door slowly opened.

This time, I was ready to attack and jumped to my feet. I figured I had nothing to lose.

This time there were two figures silhouetted in the doorway and the contrast in the size and build could not have been starker. To the left, a bear of a man, the shape of the barrel of a gun jutting out to the side. To the right, a figure at least six inches smaller, a dainty, familiar form.

'Erika?'

The bear pushed her forward and slammed the door shut. She fell to her knees. Then she stood up and jumped into my arms, tightly wrapping her arms and legs around me. I smelt her soft skin. But I also smelt her fear. Despite the excruciating pain in my ribcage, I held her for a few seconds. Then we hugged and kissed. I held her face and thanked God that she was still alive.

I hadn't realised that the chatty Russian was still in the cell. He was grinning from ear to ear.

'What have you done to her, you fucking prick?' I shouted.

He was lightning quick, and I was too slow to react as he slapped his handgun across my face. It knocked me to the floor and immediately blood dripped from my right cheekbone.

Erika fell to her knees, holding my face to hers, wiping the fresh blood from my cheek. Grimacing through the pain, I smiled and winked at her as I stumbled to my feet and nodded in the direction of the bully. 'Nice shot,' I said, fronting up to him. 'Is that the best you can do?'

'Be careful, Mr Davidson.' He was so close to me I could smell the sweat on his body. 'You are, how they say, skating on ice.'

'Thin ice, get it right.' My attitude towards these people was starting to change, and I figured that if they were indeed here to remove me of my wealth, then I was no good to them in a shallow grave. At least not yet.

'Your girlfriend is gift from the boss. She is very lucky to be alive, but now you must repay the favour. He wants something from you, understand?'

I knew exactly what he wanted.

The Russian looked Erika up and down. Grinned. 'Now I leave you alone, nature is calling.'

I took a half step forward, but Erika held my arm. 'Leave it.'

The Russian slowly backed out of the room and locked the cell door.

I turned and embraced Erika, stroking her hair as we wept together for a moment and held each other close. My heart was pounding, and I felt as though all of my troubles, just for a split second, had vanished into the dark corridor along with the gunmen. 'Are you okay?' I asked.

Nodding unconvincingly, she wiped the tears from her eyes and smiled at me, instantly melting my heart. She was so naturally beautiful, even in her distressed state.

'What did they do to you?' I asked.

'Until about half an hour ago, they just locked me in a room like this one and every so often opened the door, dropped a bottle of water, and then locked the door without saying a word.'

The relief I felt was indescribable, and I let out a huge sigh as I hugged her again. 'You have no idea how glad I am to hear that. I could only expect the worst from these sons of bitches.'

'Who are these people and what do they want?'

'They found out about the money.'

'I kind of gathered, but how?'

'I wish I knew, but they are pros, they must have contacts everywhere, maybe inside the lottery itself. Remember, I won the biggest jackpot in the world draw history, so I suppose I'm a very easy target. It's the exact reason why I didn't want to tell people in the first place.'

We walked over to the mattress and I picked up the food pouches and grabbed the tub of chocolate chip dessert.

'Get this down you,' I said. 'You need to eat.'

I sat down and talked to her while we opened up more food pouches. I told her all the detail, from the moment I had been knocked out in the car to the moment she entered my cell. I stared at the floor for a moment and then hung my head in my hands. I'd made mistakes, I knew that, and I'd been too flash and extravagant with the money. Private jets and helicopters, five-star hotels. I'd drawn attention to myself but, more importantly, to the girl I loved.

I poured my heart out and started sobbing. I was utterly ashamed of the mistakes I'd made ever since the doomed lottery win.

'You're not to blame,' Erika said. 'It's not your fault that you are a kind-hearted, generous man.'

Erika was right, of course, but that still didn't make me feel any better.

We lay on the filthy mattress in each other's arms in silence. I was so relieved, knowing she was safe next to me. We closed our eyes and drifted into a deep sleep.

42

Not a Good Day at the Office

They'd searched for hours, but to no avail. The chopper was destroyed, their agent, disguised as the captain, was dead and Davidson, the girl and all the Tycoon's tags had vanished. Not a good day at the office for Simmons and MI6.

Bissett, Minto and a few agents had returned for a briefing, and the remaining teams stayed in the vicinity of the canyon and continued to search.

'The Tycoon is in London,' Simmons announced. 'His Number Two landed in Vegas last night, which means they're still here. Minto, take Charlie Team and stick to him for the duration. Bissett, Take Delta and get to the airport. I want every tag picked up. Keep the chopper ready in case you need to move.'

43

A New Face

It was the keys rattling in the lock of the cell door that woke me, and I sat up on the mattress, my arm resting on top of Erika, who had opened her eyes too.

'You, up!' he demanded, waving a gun in my face. 'Girl stay here.'

I could feel her trembling.

'It's okay,' I whispered. 'I'm used to this by now.'

Although it broke my heart to leave Erika alone in that hellhole, I had no choice and the gunman guided me back down the dark, damp corridor and up to the open area. The doors were open again; the sunshine crept into the cave and the cool air made for a pleasant atmosphere. I concentrated hard and scanned the area outside, but unfortunately, the only thing I could see through the entrance was the red rock of the Canyon.

I was guided forcefully towards the computer desks and made to sit down. I could see the four usual Russian heavies. Two were patrolling the doorway, the chatty Russian stood beside me and I had to do a double take, as there was now a fifth person sitting at the computer station with his back to me.

The new addition was a grey-haired, aging man, wearing what looked like a smart, light cream suit. He tapped a few keys on the computer.

My heartrate began to increase as he rose from the desk and walked round towards me. There was something powerfully sinister about him. As I scanned his face, he removed his sunglasses and greeted me in an accent much closer to home. 'Good morning, Mr Davidson. I trust our hosts are treating you well?'

He was British, quite distinguished, with an aristocratic air about him.

'Fantastic,' I replied sarcastically.

'Excellent news. Now, let me fill you in with a few details. Listen carefully and please, keep any questions until I've finished.'

Before I had a chance to answer, he turned on his heels, placed his hands behind his back, cleared his throat and continued. 'On Saturday, 19 December, you were the lucky winner of the World Lottery. You visited Lottery HQ alone, where they confirmed that you, Mr Mark Davidson, were in possession of the record winning ticket. From here you spent the next three days at the La Mercia Hotel, where you dined the first evening at the hotel's exclusive restaurant and spent the remaining time in room 31, with the young lady whom I allowed to join you in your room last night.'

It was at that point he paused and smiled at me, waiting for maybe appreciation or a positive reaction.

'Oh wow, yes, thank you so much for the piss and lice-infected mattress in my prison cell. It was so comfortable, better than the La Mercia Hotel.'

He ignored my injection of humour. 'You then headed out to New York City, spending Christmas Eve at the New York Plaza and Christmas Day at the Bellagio Villas, where you experienced the darker side of Vegas.'

He reached into his rear trouser pocket and produced a chain, throwing it in my direction. It landed on my lap and I grabbed it before it fell to the floor.

I frowned, staring at the necklace in my right hand as an icy shiver crept down my spine. 'I don't understand?'

'I'm sorry, Mr Davidson, the two clowns who assaulted you were only meant to force you into a vehicle waiting to drive you to this little cave of mine. They were well paid for what should have been one minute's work, but unfortunately, they became greedy when they spotted your girlfriend's necklace and they didn't know who they were dealing with. They thought they could disappear into the night without fulfilling our agreement.'

I couldn't believe what I was hearing. How long had they been following me?

'You see, Mark, I work for an organisation that, well, simply does not tolerate that kind of behaviour. Let's cut a long and rather messy story short. The two thieves' various body parts are now buried somewhere in this rocky desert. I took the liberty of retrieving your necklace - I am, of course, a gentleman and understand the effort you made with your lovely girlfriend.'

He smiled again. Why would he give the necklace back if he was going to kill us? What sort of mind games was he playing?

He pulled up a chair from the computer table and perched just in front of me. He sat back, crossed his left leg over his right, and continued. 'It's very simple, Mark. Very simple indeed. You give me exactly what I want and you and your girl walk away and get on with your lives. If you don't give me what I want … well, let's just say you will be joining the greedy men out there in the desert somewhere.

'Why don't you just get to the point and I will see if I might be able to help you?'

'I'm sure you have guessed by now. I want the lottery money.' He stared at me, smirking, and let the silence linger.

'You son of a bitch, how do you think you can get away with all of this? You can't go around kidnapping people and threatening them like this. Who the hell do you think you are?'

He stopped me mid-sentence, holding his hand up towards my face. 'Mark, Mark, Mark. You see, that's exactly what I have done and will do, unless you do what I tell you. My organisation needs to remove the money from you. I'm afraid and that is the reason I've flown five thousand miles today.'

Standing, he turned and nodded to the chief Russian thug.

'Up, Mr Davidson, let's go,' he said as he marched me from the centre of the room towards the large table of computer screens. He dumped me down hard onto the plastic chair. He stood one step backwards and pointed his gun at my head.

He cocked the weapon.

44

Untraceable accounts

I knew he wasn't about to fire. I was beginning to get the measure of these thugs. I turned my head and smiled at him. I was growing in confidence. They needed me. It was as simple as that.

The table was filled with a multitude of computer screens and my Russian friend had slammed me into a chair in front of a corner area with six large black screens spread out over three tables.

The first two screens displayed stock markets from around the world and flashed with ever changing numbers of share prices. In the bottom right corner of the second screen was a live feed of a stock exchange floor, with hundreds of people milling around a room, buying and selling stocks and shares.

The third and fourth screens displayed various air traffic control systems and flight paths, and as far as I could tell, they were currently tracking a number of aircraft over the US and the UK.

The fifth monitor was the screen that took me by surprise. It displayed a full listing of my private information; bank accounts, passport details, credit card numbers, names and addresses of family, friends, ex-colleagues. You name it; it was on display.

The last monitor was open at my new bank account's homepage and would no doubt be the screen that I would use for this stage of our chat.

'Mark,' the old guy smiled, 'here is how this will work. As long as you follow these very simple and clear instructions, this time tomorrow you will be back at the hotel and this will all seem like a bad dream.'

He strolled over to screen, tapping the top corner with his finger and smiled at me. His surgically enhanced, million-dollar smile beamed in the daylight.

'You will log into your new bank account and we will take a little look at your balance. Then, you will call your 24-hour account management team and request an immediate account transfer to this account number.' He handed me a small slip of paper.

Printed on it was a strange-looking sort code and account number. In the top right-hand corner of the slip was a small emblem and 'Cayman Islands Bank' written underneath.

'So we are clear and you understand the position. Once the money hits this account, it will be immediately transferred to ten numbered accounts, each in a different country. Once the money hits those ten accounts, the process will repeat at various stages over the next 24 hours. These accounts are untraceable, Mark, as I'm sure you will have already gathered. The organisations I work with are very good at covering their tracks.'

He stood directly behind me, both hands on my shoulders, and bent over to speak into my ear in a cruel, deliberate whisper. 'Once the transfers are complete, the cave will be emptied and you are free to go. You are 20 miles or so from a helipad. Fit guys like you and your girlfriend should easily cover that distance in a day.'

Nice and simple, I thought as I stared at the homepage. I transfer all of my money, you simply hide it and walk away without a trace. Am I supposed to just sit here and allow this to happen and believe this man will let us walk away?

He walked back to the screens. 'This is a very simple transaction and completely painless if you follow the instructions. Log into your account and let us have a look at the balance.' He tapped the top of the monitor and strolled towards the far end of the long tables. The screen went black as the chatty Russian passed me a keyboard.

'Good boy,' he said and chuckled, waving his gun in my face.

'Prick,' I said under my breath and clicked one of the keys to wake up the computer. I had little choice. I input the two sets of account numbers, logged into my bank, and accessed the password screens. I entered the three different passwords which were needed to access my main account and was eventually directed to my homepage. There, on the right, was my current account balance: £245,489,891.66.

Up to this point, the vast fortune had not seemed real, but as I ogled the huge balance, the pit of my stomach heaved as it all sank in. All of my hopes and dreams were about to be destroyed. Possibly worse. Why was this happening to me? How the hell was this happening to me? Erika and I had planned to travel the world and enjoy the rest of our lives together, and now I was about to have everything ripped away as fast as it landed in the account in the first place.

As instructed, I wrote the exact balance on the piece of paper that the old bastard had given me and handed it to him. I slouched back in the seat and hurled the keyboard on the table.

'Very good, Mark. You have not been wasteful with your cash, which is good to see. Now, let's go.' He pointed his finger towards the large open doors.

'Go? Go where?' I got to my feet. The Russian, who had placed his handgun in the waist of his trousers, was now pointing his machine gun at me.

'There is a call to be made,' the old man replied as he guided me towards the exit.

45

Tyre Tracks in the Sand

'Sir, this is Bravo. We are approximately three clicks from the chopper wreckage site. I think we have found something.'

The Bravo team leader was on the secure com to the conference room, where Simmons and a few of the MI6 team were coordinating movements.

'What is it, Bravo?'

'Tyre tracks, sir. A shit load of them. Uploading the video now, sir.'

The upload took a few minutes, but there they were. Tracks all over the sand and leading off north.

'Get your fucking arses mobile and follow those fucking tracks, Bravo.'

46

A Question of Trust

We walked outside; the sunlight beaming down on my face. I inhaled a few long, deep breaths and gazed out into the vast expanse of land. The view was so different in the daylight and portrayed the magnitude of the red, rocky canyon. Misshapen rock dominated the area, and I noticed, glancing back to my prison, that we were situated on the canyon floor itself, with a large overhang of rock directly above us, acting as a perfect cover for the makeshift hideout.

The tyre marks of the armoured vehicle were visible on the floor in front of us and stretched for 100 yards or so out into the open, before simply vanishing because of the crosswinds across the path of the cave.

The old guy approached and handed over his mobile phone. 'The number of the bank is stored on the phone. Just press the green button twice and you will be connected with your account team. Tell them you wish to transfer two hundred and forty-five million pounds into this account number and, as I'm feeling generous, you can keep the change left. Call it a late Christmas gift, shall we?'

More mind games. Was he serious, leaving me so much money? It made no sense, unless he was trying to convince me he was going to let us go. He handed me a slip of paper with the account details and at that moment nothing would have given me greater pleasure than to drop the mobile phone on the floor, stamp my full weight of authority on it and slap the son of a bitch in front of me.

'If they start asking questions, such as why you're moving the money or whether you prefer to visit the branch and discuss it, simply refuse and stick to the plan. Tell them you are moving the money as you are moving to the Cayman Islands. Simple, easy and it will put a halt to any more questions. This is your money, Mark. And they are at the other end of the line to advise you, nothing more. Once they confirm everything with you, it will take 24 hours to transfer the full amount and then, well … you're free to go. How easy is that?'

He smiled at me as if this was all a simple game of chess and he had just made his check and mate, and my reward for obedience was staying alive.

'What's stopping you from killing me once I transfer the money?'

The question had jumped from my lips without me thinking of the consequences. But I was right. What was stopping these people from shooting me right here in this cave once I had transferred the money? They could do the same with Erika and bury us both in the dirt.

'Nothing, I guess,' he said. 'I suppose you will need to trust me, Mark. I'm a man of my word. If I really wanted to, then your girlfriend would be dead now. You would be minus a few fingers and this could be turning out to be your worst nightmare, far worse than the one you are living right now. I'm a gentleman and that is not the way I do business. The organisation is very professional and we have simple philosophies. We have done this more than once, Mark. Have you heard of any lottery winners turning up dead lately? Let's just get through this and I promise you, you will live to tell the tale.'

Under different circumstances, the panoramic views in front of me would have been breath-taking. But at that moment, I would have given anything to be back at my parents' house, penniless, in front of the large open fire.

I looked at the nameless face and prayed that he was a man of his word. 'Okay, let's start.'

'Very good, Mark. Now please, if you can call the bank and tell them to transfer the money from your account to the numbered account. After this, you are on your way home.'

I sighed, shaking my head in defeat, and glanced at his phone. Two choices were presenting themselves to me, both of which had disappointing endings. I either transferred the money and hoped that they would leave, or refuse and risk being shot, my body dumped in this desert.

I double-clicked the green button, and it dialled directly to my bank. An account manager answered within a few seconds. 'Hi, this is Marlene. How may I help you?' she said in a pleasant tone.

'Hi Marlene, this is Mark Davidson. Can I give you my account numbers, please?'

'Certainly Mr Davidson, please go ahead.'

I gave her my account numbers and also the three passwords, as well as confirming a full list of personal details.

'Thank you, Mr Davidson, everything is in order. How may I help you?'

Taking a long, deep breath and steadying myself for a trail of lies, I began the drawn-out process that would wipe out all of my hopes and dreams for the future.

'I would like to make a transfer, please.'

'Certainly Mr Davidson, how much would you like to transfer and to which numbered account please?'

'Two hundred and forty-five million Pounds.'

The line went quiet for a second. 'Erm, okay sir, the transfer will take some time and I will need you to complete all the transfer documents.'

'If you can email them to me now please, I will complete them and send them straight back to you.'

'I will also need the bank manager to call and confirm before the transfer is carried out.'

I thought for a second, glancing over to my attentive audience who, for an amusing few seconds, had a slight panic in their eyes.

'It's fine. When I've sent the documents, I will call you straight back to confirm and then you can put him on the phone.'

'That will be fine, sir. The documents will arrive momentarily,' she replied. 'Goodbye, Mr Davidson.'

'Goodbye.'

The line went dead and the old guy took the phone from me. He removed the earpiece from his left ear. 'Very good, Mark.' He smirked. 'Let's get the paperwork complete and then one more call to the bank and you are home free.'

They took me back into the cave and pushed me in front of the computer screens, where I logged into my email account and opened the email which had already arrived from the bank.

The printers were set to work and the documentation spat out onto the desk. The old guy checked the paperwork carefully. After almost twenty minutes,, he laid it out in front of me to complete. I complied, completed every form, and signed at all the relevant places.

My new best friend watched closely. 'Almost there,' he said, taking the papers from me as he scanned every page into the computer.

'Thanks for destroying my life. You know won't get away with this, right?'

'Oh but you're wrong, Mark. We will get away with this. We have before and we will again. You have no idea what this organisation is capable of, so please, let's just finish off the business and make the final call.'

I emailed the documents directly to the bank with a note to say I would call back in a few minutes. And then a reflection on the screen of the computer chilled me to the bone.

I took a deep breath. Now I knew my fate, I knew both our fates.

I glanced at the screen again. The files confirmed the direct transfer of most of my remaining balance to a numbered account in the Cayman Islands.

We were in touching distance of ending any dream that Erika and I had planned together. But what choice did I have when five madmen were circling and ready to do whatever it took to get their hands on my money?

The old man smiled. 'The documents are sent. Now let's go and make the final call, shall we?'

I was subsequently dragged from my chair and marched out of the entrance. The old man handed me his phone.

'You son of a bitch, you have no intention of letting us go, do you?'

'I've already told you, Mark, when this is over, you will be left here to find your way home. Now please, make the call.'

His tone was serious and somehow sincere, but I was convinced the chatty Russian had other ideas. His reflection on the computer screen pointed at me and then dragged his finger across his throat.

'Bullshit, as soon as you get the money, you will leave us to the mercy of these monkeys.'

'You will make this bloody call!' The old man raised his voice, his eyes bulging. 'Do not push me.'

I took forward a step so our faces were almost touching. Within a split second, a machine gun pointed directly at me. 'Fuck you,' I whispered through gritted teeth.

The old man looked at me and strangely, he smiled and turned on the spot, put his right hand into his pocket, removed what looked like a mint and popped it into his mouth. He glanced to my right and said something in Russian. One of the heavies turned and walked back inside the cave.

'Oh, Mark. I really didn't want it to be this way, but you have left me no choice. You have done all the hard work and you now only need to finish with a simple phone call. Please tell me, why do you want to be such a hero?'

'I've nothing to lose. Once the money has been transferred, we will die.'

'Whatever do you mean? I set the rules, Mark. This outcome has been planned for. You will not be harmed if you follow my instructions. At the moment, you are trying to defer from the plan and that, Mark, is simply unacceptable.'

As he finished his sentence, I heard a scream and turned towards the exit to see the chatty Russian dragging Erika out of the cave by her hair.

'No!' I screamed and started to run towards her, but the two other heavies scurried in front of her, guns raised, and blocked me from reaching her. She was forced to her knees as she pleaded with them to stop.

One of them pulled out his handgun and pressed the barrel against her forehead, his arm stretched, ready to shoot.

'Please,' she screamed. 'No, please!'

'Leave her alone,' I shouted and turned to the old man who had not flinched. 'Why are you doing this, please?'

'I am not doing this, Mark. This is you, you are doing this. You will make this call or you will watch her die. Here, now.'

'Okay please, leave her out of this.' I had no doubt they were planning to kill us both regardless, but I could not watch her die in front of me.

He pointed to the phone still in my hand. 'Then you know what to do.'

'Call off the dogs. You don't need to have a gun to her head, please. I'll make your damn call.'

The old man nodded once. The Russian lowered his weapon and backed away from Erika.

I lifted the phone and double-clicked the green button.

Again, I answered the security questions, and the girl asked me to hold the line while she put me through to the manager.

'Mr Davidson, how are you today, sir?'

'I'm just fantastic,' I answered sarcastically.

'We received your documents for transferring to a numbered account at the bank of Cayman, correct, sir?' he asked.

I froze. This is it. My money is gone. 'That's … that's correct.'

'All the documents are present and correct, Mr Davidson. I will begin the transfer process immediately. May I ask why you are transferring the funds, sir?

I stared at Erika, who was still on her knees and was now looking straight at me, tears streaming down her face. She must have wondered what the hell I was talking about.

'I'm moving to the Cayman Islands next week and it will be easier for me to control my funds from that bank. I have a meeting with the bank manager soon after I arrive, so if you could begin the transfer immediately, I would appreciate it.' I took a deep breath and prayed that he would just accept my reasoning and let me go.

'Of course sir, I've already authorised the transfer although it will take up to 24 hours to complete. We have your email address and your contact numbers, so should we need anything we will be in touch. I would like to take this opportunity to thank you for banking with us and would appreciate it if you would pop into the branch before you leave for the Cayman Islands, just for a general chat, if that's okay.'

'Sure, no problem and thanks for your help.'

I dropped the phone from my ear and rushed over to Erika. I picked her up from the ground. 'I'm sorry,' I whispered to her. 'I'm so sorry for everything.'

'You see, that was not so difficult, Mark. Was it?' the old man said as he walked over to where Erika and I were standing. 'You can relax now. You now get to spend the next 24 hours together in your cosy room while we wait for the transfer to complete. When everything is in order, I will keep my side of the bargain and you will be released unharmed.'

I knew differently.

We were escorted to the room by one of the heavies, shoved into the cell and the door was locked behind us.

I grabbed Erika and hugged her tightly. 'Oh my God, I'm so sorry. Are you okay?'

She looked pale, frightened, and like she was running out of steam. I took her by the hand and walked over to the mattress and sat down. I told her about the emails, the phone calls and all about the new mystery man. 'I'm so sorry,' I said over and over again.

'It's only money and we are still alive. Let's be thankful for that, at least.'

I hung my head between my legs, feeling completely overwhelmed by all the events that had led to this point. I was always the one to believe in fate or believe that things were meant to be, but winning this money had brought me to this unbelievable place and in the next 24 hours there was every possibility we were going to die.

Fate had just dealt us a crushing blow, and I still needed to tell Erika what I'd seen on the computer screen. 'I've got something else to tell you,' I managed to say without completely breaking down, wiping tears from my face and turning towards her.

'What else could there possibly be to top this?' she replied.

'The Russian, I saw something when they had me on a computer.' I stopped mid-sentence, frightened to actually hear the words from my own lips. 'Oh my God, what have I done?' I hung my head back down into my hands, trying to hide my face.

'What's wrong, Mark? What did you see?'

My voice lowered as I finished the sentence, and she slowly turned her head away.

She sobbed hard into her hands. I felt ashamed, and I stood up and walked towards the doorway. I punched the wooden door, turned, and leaned backward, raising both my hands to my head. 'It's not supposed to be this way,' I shouted, kicking the door and cursing what these people were doing to us. 'What's the problem with wanting to be happy?'

'Come here.' Erika urged me to sit down next to her. 'You might be mistaken, they might just let us go'

'Why would they? In 24 hours we won't be needed. We know too much. We've seen their faces, which means we could ID them.'

I was defensive and angry, and Erika could sense it. She was trying to keep the situation as positive as she could and I was the one losing the plot.

'So I suppose all we can do now is wait and hope,' she said.

'Maybe not,' I said. 'We could always try to get out of here.'

47

A Plan

I stood up from the mattress and paced the floor as Erika glanced at me with a concerned expression. 'Get out of here?' she asked. 'How on earth are we going to do that when we're locked in this tiny hole?'

'Listen,' I replied quietly, walking over and kneeling in front of her. She was still shaking.

'I think our best, in fact, our only chance of getting out of here is to hit one of the heavies when they come through that door.'

'But they've got guns, Mark. How can we do anything with one of those pointing straight at us?'

As she stared at me, directly into my eyes, I felt ultimately responsible for her life. I was beginning to think from a military point of view. After all, it was me who brought her into this mess in the first place.

'I think we've got a chance,' I repeated, walking over to the large wooden entrance, slamming it with my hand. I turned around. 'Okay, so picture this; one of the heavies unlocks the door and I am standing here.' I stood to the left of the doorway with my back to the wall. 'Now, the door opens like this from the outside.' I motioned the door opening. 'I'm hidden from view and the gunman instinctively looks at the mattress, right?'

'Okay.'

'It opens slightly every time. He is cautious if he thinks both of us are there. He will lower the gun, he feels safe, we are too far away from him to pose any sort of threat. And gotcha.'

My tone and pace started to speed up, and I stood in front of the door now, mimicking the heavy entering our room. I was looking at her hoping, hoping my enthusiasm will rub off on her, but her facial expression had not changed.

'That's our chance,' I continued, 'our only chance. That's when he is vulnerable. The split second the door swings fully open and he takes just one step. If I can time it right and swing this heavy door just as hard as I can, I'll squash him like a fly and we can grab his gun.'

I was pacing the door area now, adrenaline pumping through my veins as I replayed over and over in my head how I visualised the scene. 'He won't see a thing and if I can slam the door as soon as the gun starts to come through the door, then he will be slammed into the door frame.'

Erika was shaking her head. 'Guns, Mark. Guns and Russian mafia, it's all so alien to me. How are we going to get away with it?'

I went to her and wrapped my arms around her for a moment. I released her and held her face with my hands and kissed her softly. 'We haven't got a choice, Erika.'

'I know, I know.' She sounded defeated.

We had to try, we agreed. It was our only hope. 'He might just shoot us both,' she murmured.

'I'm nervous about the whole thing as well, but if the Russian bully is right, then the next visitor to our room could be here to stick a bullet in our heads. I'm not going to sit here and die without a fight; this is the only chance we will have.'

We curled up on the mattress, and she began to stroke my hair. I closed my eyes and tried to clear my mind, which proved extremely difficult as the scenario of the Russian heavy sticking his hand through the door with his gun replayed over and over in my mind.

'Sex!' Erika exclaimed as she sat up suddenly.

'I beg your pardon.'

'Sex,' she repeated. 'I've been thinking … if he comes into the room and can't physically see you, then he'll be on his guard until at least he knows where you are.'

'Agreed.'

'But if he can't see you, and he can hear you …'

'Genius, bloody genius, so you'll be under the blanket with some of my clothes to pack it out and –'

'I'll be under there making early orgasm sounds and he'll have no reason to think you are anywhere but under those blankets, too.'

I jumped up from the mattress, almost sending Erika flying, and scanned the room as if preparing for a fight. 'It'll work, of course it will work.'

'It has to,' she said.

We kissed and went through the plan again.

Later, when Erika was asleep, I got up and took up my position behind the door.

Alone with my thoughts, I thought about my life and how I came to be sitting in this cold, damp hellhole. What did I ever do to deserve this? Thinking back to a few weeks ago when I had found the lottery ticket in my kitchen, I remember how happy I'd felt, knowing that my life was going to change forever. If I never found the ticket or won the damned lottery, where would I be right now? Would I have asked Erika out on a date or would the unconfident Mark Davidson still be sitting alone in his cold flat, alone and unemployed?

Even though that sounded dull and slightly pathetic, it was certainly a million miles away from my current situation. Thinking about fate or things that were meant to be made me realise maybe I was never meant to win the jackpot. Maybe on that cold and snowy morning, I was never destined to visit the store where I purchased the winning ticket. I'd experienced the money for such a short length of time and now it was gone. Not only that, but there was every possibility that in the next few hours, I would die where I sat.

What about my parents and my family? What about Erika's family? She'd been unwillingly dragged into this shocking state of affairs and as she lay peacefully on the mattress, I would have given anything to allow her a safe passage home, even if it meant sacrificing myself.

I couldn't begin to comprehend what my family would go through if they were to find out I had been murdered. Not only that, but I was murdered because of a jackpot win that I didn't even inform them of. Then again, if we were buried in the middle of the Nevada desert, they would never know if I was alive or dead.

Maybe if I had been honest from the beginning, then all the media attention and fame would have frightened these terrorists away from me. How stupid and selfish I'd been trying to keep everything to myself. What had I hoped to achieve? To keep the media out of our lives for a short while and tell a load of lies to everyone for the rest of my life?

I felt myself getting upset and took a few deep breaths. Whatever happens, I will not let Erika simply die like this. I will do everything in my power to make sure she gets back to her family. I whispered to myself, 'You can do this. Just stick to the plan and take him by surprise. Remember your training. You can do this.'

But then I thought about what would happen afterwards. Would I simply knock him out or would I have to shoot him? Would I have the balls to shoot a man in cold blood after I'd disarmed him?

My training and little experience of war zones prepared me as best they I could. I would have to do it if there was the remotest of possibilities of getting out alive.

Questions came and went. Could I really pull the trigger and expose Erika to such extreme violence? I asked myself the same question over and over again, picturing the whole scene many times.

48

Coffee Break

'Are you getting this, sir?'

Bravo team had sent a live feed of a large cave entrance with two men dressed in desert camouflage suits and carrying machine guns. The team was a good mile from away from the cave entrance and kept their distance to await for further instruction.

'Bissett, get that chopper in the air. Alpha, Charlie, Delta teams, get to Bravo's position and hold.'

Simmons's fifth expresso was kicking in. His emotions were running riot. He knew this would be the only chance they would get. This was it. A major haul of the Tycoon's team in one hit was within reach.

49

Action Stations

I'd paced the floor with my thoughts for what seemed like hours. I drank a little of the water that we had left. My mouth was dry, my head was pounding, and I was tired beyond comprehension.

Erika lay still on the mattress and the only noise I could hear was from her breathing deeply as she slept.

As I walked past the door towards my hiding place to do yet one more roleplay, my heart almost skipped a beat as I heard the clunk of a key from outside the door. My body started to shake as the adrenaline returned, pumping violently through my veins as I dived quickly towards the mattress to give Erika a shake. As her eyes flickered open, I dashed back to the wall behind the door. I took a long, slow breath and held it as the key started to turn in the lock.

I had no time to think, no time to plan, no time to ask myself if I should react now or wait. I was frozen to the spot and found myself staring at the door, waiting and watching for the slightest movement.

My stomach went into spasm as the key turned in the lock and then stopped. I heard Erika moaning, clearly the guard did too. I looked over at the mattress. Erika's beautiful thigh was exposed and her moaning was increasing. She was putting in a decent acting performance, so much so that I wished I had been under the blanket with her.

It happened in the blink of an eye.

The door slowly opened and on cue a silenced handgun peered through the gap, then a hand and the lower portion of an arm. He chuckled. 'You filthy English pigs,' he called out and finally took a step forward, so that his body lingered in the doorway.

This was it, no turning back. I waited until I could see his arm and his shoulder and with all my might, all of my love, my hate, my anger and my fear, I slammed my right shoulder as hard as I could into the heavy wooden door.

I heard his bones crush and his skin, muscles and sinew rip apart as the door smashed into his arm just above the elbow. He screamed as the gun fell to the floor and, taking no chances, I took a hold of his wrist and pulled it hard towards me. I snapped his wrist and forearm like dry twigs and dived to the floor to pick up the weapon. I jumped to my feet, pulled the door open fully, and dragged the guard to the middle of the cell.

My heart was beating out of my chest and as I pointed the gun directly at the Russian's head, I noticed a machine gun strapped tightly around his back. Judging by the state of his arm, which now hung at a grotesque angle by his side, there was no way he could even get to the gun, let alone fire it.

'Up,' I said, kicking his leg and standing back from where he was sprawled on the floor.

Beyond this point was where my planning ceased, so I needed to get him tied up and gagged and think pretty fast about what was going to happen next.

He was grimacing with pain, struggled to his knees, and then he stood.

Pointing the gun towards him, I turned to close the door. As I reached the door I took my eyes off him for a split second and heard a bloodcurdling shriek. It was Erika screaming a warning and as I turned around, the Russian was hurtling through the air towards me.

Without thinking, without hesitating and just before he hit me, I pulled the trigger of the large black gun. It all happened in slow motion. The bullet hit him in the forehead, blood instantly erupting from the back of his head as small fragments of bone flew onto the wall behind him. His huge torso hit me in the chest and bundled me into the door.

As he lay on top of me, his eyes were open and a look of fear was still visible on his face. His body shuddered for a few seconds.

Erika jumped up and ran over to me. I rolled away from the Russian, and she fell on me, wrapping her arms around my neck. She was shaking wildly as her chest started to spasm and she lost control of her breathing.

I held her face in my hands. 'Breath Erika, breathe with me,' I said. 'It's okay, it was him or us, think of that.'

She inhaled slowly, held her breath for a second, and then released it and I urged her to keep repeating the process three or four times.

I stared at the gun and then at the dead body on the floor.

'I shot him,' I managed to say, still in shock, 'I actually shot him.'

'It was self-defence.'

'I know.'

I surprised myself just how comfortable I was with shooting a man dead. The body was still, blood oozing from the rear of his head onto the floor.

I looked at Erika. 'We have a chance, but we need to figure this out,' I said.

'What do you mean?'

'He was obviously sent here to fetch us or to kill us, so I guess we have maybe five minutes to think of a plan before the cavalry is sent in.'

I squatted over the body and held my breath as I removed the large machine gun hanging around his mangled arm and shoulder. I handed the handgun to Erika.

'No,' she said meekly.

I held my hand over hers as she unwillingly took the weapon.

'You're staying here for the next ten minutes. I need to see if there's a way out of here. Just point and pull the trigger at anyone other than me who walks through that door.'

'Just shoot! I … I can't … what do I do? I can't do it—'

'Baby please,' I said firmly, 'we don't have time. We need to act. We've got a matter of minutes before another member of his crew appears.'

Without waiting for an answer, I took her hand and pointed the gun at the door. I walked back to the body, took another deep breath, and bent down to check his pockets. I found a bunch of keys and a small wallet in his trouser pockets and his mobile phone in a jacket pocket.

50

Trained to Kill

Without hesitation I flipped open the handset of the phone and dialled 911.

After a few seconds, the phone beeped three times and then there was nothing. Confused, I looked at the display. 'No service. We get this close and then no fucking service!' I was about to launch the phone at the wall when Erika grabbed my arm.

'No! Don't smash it. We might use it later. If we actually get out of here, we will need to call the police.'

'You're right, sorry, yes, I know.' I was stuttering and tried to gather my thoughts as Erika took the phone and put it into her pocket.

'Police!' Something had just dawned on me. 'Of course.'

'What do you mean "of course"?'

I pulled my wallet from my back pocket and opened it. I rummaged around and found the detective Simmons' business card.

'Simmons?' Erika said.

'Yes, he's the detective who dealt with us at the robbery, remember? He gave me his card at the hospital.' I stored his number on the phone and attempted to make the call, which failed because of the lack of mobile coverage. 'When we get some service, just click the call button twice and the call will be made.'

I handed the phone back to Erika, who pocketed it and placed both hands nervously back on the gun. I guessed we had a minute or two now before another heavy was sent to find out what was taking the dead one so long. 'I need to check the corridor. We can't stay in here, it's too risky. Stay in the corner on the mattress and try not to look at that,' I said, pointing to the lifeless body. 'I'll be one minute, I promise; I just need to make sure the coast is clear, okay?'

We kissed, and I closed my eyes, trying not to think too much about the situation.

'Please hurry,' she said, walking towards the mattress. She sat on the edge and I guessed she would desperately try not to stare at the room's new edition.

Another deep breath and I gently opened the large wooden door, gradually raising my arm and pointing the gun out in front of me. I peered my head around to the left of the door. Nothing.

I stepped out and locked the door, quickly turning to face forwards. Glancing back into the darkness, I could see no movement and let a breath out slowly as I walked into the unknown. I took a few steps away from our prison cell and scanned the rest of the corridor. Although quite dark, I could see enough to make my way slowly forwards. Other than my footsteps, there was complete silence as I inched down it, the gun still pointing out in front of me. At the end of the corridor, there was another door. I figured it must have been the room in which they held Erika whilst I was questioned. I turned back around and scanned the area in front of me, noticing that every ten yards there was a large column which supported the ceiling above us. I approached the first one and stood behind it with my back to the rocky wall.

Perhaps it would be possible to hide here and wait for the next heavy to come down. I stepped back onto the pathway, gradually making my way up the corridor towards our room. As I stopped outside the door, I caught a glimpse of a figure in the distance out of the corner of my right eye. I froze for a second and then saw another large column three feet down the corridor. I turned my back on it and inched backwards in the darkness. I was now four feet or so from our cell, but with the approaching figure working his way towards me, I could not take the chance of getting caught trying to open the door.

'Shit,' I whispered under my breath. What the hell was I going to do?

The adrenaline kicked in again. I gripped onto the gun tightly and steadied myself. I made sure the silencer was secured tightly to the end and the safety clip was set to off.

The footsteps skulked towards me, growing closer and closer, louder and louder. Holding my breath, I slowly lifted the gun up towards my chest.

'Drakov!' the man called out.

His footsteps grew louder until they echoed on top of me. I froze, held my breath and leaned as close as possible into the edging of the column. His large machine gun slowly appeared in front of me, pointing directly down the corridor, and then he stopped. I could see half of the gun and as I glanced down, I spotted one of his feet pointing in the same direction.

I was convinced he could hear my heart pounding as he stood completely still for what seemed like an eternity. Then he turned, slowly continuing to walk until he eventually had his back to me. He edged further away towards our cell. I slowly leaned forward just far enough to see him stop at the door.

I let my breath escape. A million thoughts rushed around my head as I tried to visualise the next thirty seconds. Erika was locked inside with the dead Russian and the moment the new heavy walked into the room and saw what had happened, she would be shot. Or she would manage to shoot him first.

I could not let either situation unfold.

The Russian lowered the machine gun for a second and rummaged through his pocket, searching for the key to the room.

It was now or never.

I slowly raised my weapon and moved forward quietly. My right hand was shaking slightly as the Russian removed the keys from his pocket and moved towards the door. Taking a second step forward as he placed the key into the lock, I aimed directly for the back of his skull and, without thinking, pressed the trigger of the gun.

A single bullet flew out of the chamber and lodged in the rear of his head. He didn't make a sound as the bullet penetrated his skull and sent him slamming instantly to the ground. I released my breath slowly. I stood perfectly still, pointing my gun at the Russian's body, looking for any signs of life.

Then I took a few steps and grimaced at the sight. I tried not to vomit as I witnessed the blood and small fragments of brain trickling out of his skull. I grabbed his machine gun and wrapped the strap over my shoulder. I opened the door slowly. The first dead Russian lay where he'd fell, a huge pool of blood now covering the surrounding area. I looked up. Erika was standing in the corner of the room with a handgun pointing directly at me.

As soon as she saw me, she dropped the gun and ran over to me, grabbing me around the neck. 'Are you okay? Where did you go?'

I moved to the left of the door to reveal the second body lying in the corridor.

'Oh my God.' She started shaking, her teeth chattering.

'It was him or you.' I gripped her firmly, lifting her chin to look into her eyes. 'Do you hear me, Erika?'

She started crying. 'I can't believe this is happening.'

'I know, but we need to get going.' I held her tight. 'Breathe.' When her shaking subsided somewhat, I said, 'We have another body and another bloke who won't be returning, which means in a few minutes the rest of the clan is going to be seriously suspicious. We can't just sit and wait anymore; we need to get out of here and we need to go now.'

Erika held open the door open as I dragged the second body into the room. He must have weighed

15 or 16 stone, so it took rather a lot of effort to pull him into the room with us.

I left him face down near his dead friend and searched his pockets. Again, I found a mobile phone which I tucked into the front of my pocket. I also found another handgun.

'You want the machine gun or the smaller one?' I asked Erika, kissing her forehead. 'I love you,' I said. 'I've always loved you and I will always love you. We are going to get through this.'

'I love you too and I want to go home. I don't want any bloody guns.' She put her hands over her eyes and let out a low wail.

'Erika, listen to me, keep the handgun. It could make all the difference.'

She nodded slowly and took a step forward. This was completely alien to her. Unlike me, she had never even held a gun, let alone fired one.

I grabbed at her hand and she squeezed behind me as we edged out of the room and back into the dark corridor. I turned quickly, locked the cell door behind me and threw the keys into the darkness.

'Stay close to this wall,' I whispered. We stopped at every large column, breathing deeply while checking the top of the corridor before moving on. Fortunately, the corridor was dark and quite long, which allowed us to stay undetected as we headed slowly towards the top.

As we approached the fourth column, I whispered to Erika to stop. The light above us was out completely. We were standing in total darkness. I leaned forward, glanced up the corridor and immediately shot backwards against the wall.

'Fuck.'

'What?'

'Another one,' I said under my breath. 'Just stay hard against the wall, hold your breath when he gets near, and whatever you do, don't move.'

51

Airborne

'All teams in place, sir.'

The Bravo team leader announced that Alpha, Bravo, Charlie and Delta teams were in position. Approximately one mile from the cave, the teams were ready to begin their team descent.

'Bissett, how long?' Simmons asked

'Twenty minutes give or take,' she replied. 'The chopper is airborne and on its way to their position.'

52

Problems with Reception

Her body tightened as she pressed hard against the wall and leaned against my side. I'd forgotten about the pain in my ribs for a few seconds, but as she leaned into me, she pushed hard on my ribcage and I almost let out a gasp as the sharp pain shot down my left side.

I took a long hard breath and angled myself slightly back down the corridor towards our cell, away from the oncoming Russian.

'Drakov ... Matvi ...' The third Russian was strolling purposefully down the corridor, calling out the names of his two associates.

His footsteps grew louder and Erika pushed hard against me, increasing the intensity of pain in my left side. I bit my lip so hard that I felt a small pop in the skin as my teeth sank in. I tasted blood.

We couldn't see a thing in the darkness, but I could now hear him breathing as he passed directly in front of us.

'Drakov!' he shouted again.

We were frozen to the spot and Erika's heartbeat raced against my body as he took another few steps forwards. I had my left arm wrapped around her, holding her as tightly as possible and trying desperately not to move a muscle. I kept my eyes focused on where the darkness met the light on the floor.

Keep walking, keep walking, I urged the Russian on. Another step, then another, and then I spotted a dim shadow appearing on the ground.

Slowly, I used my left hand to hold on to Erika's shoulder and gently pulled myself forward, inching my right arm upward in the direction of the Russian. A final step and he was now visible in the light, creeping forwards as he scanned left and right, looking for any clue as to the whereabouts of the other heavies. I took a long, deep breath and stepped forward onto the cobbles. My foot landed on a small stone and my shoe made a slight scraping noise against the hard cobble.

The Russian spun around.

Fortunately, I was still in darkness and he couldn't react quickly enough and for the third time that day, I killed a man.

The bullet coasted into his forehead and his head jerked back, lifting him off his feet for a split second before he crashed back to the ground.

A muffled scream came from behind me. Quickly and quietly, I rushed over to the Russian, whose body was shaking violently. Although the bullet had connected with his head, he was still alive and spitting blood from his mouth.

Without thinking and without hesitating, I pointed the gun towards his temple and pulled the trigger again. The groaning and shaking stopped instantly.

I edged back towards Erika. 'Are you okay?'

'No,' she replied, 'are you?'

'No,' I answered, 'but better than him, I suppose.'

We left the Russian where he was and crept back to the other side of the corridor.

'We can't stop,' I said quietly. 'We need to keep going and try to find our way out of here. The chatty Russian and the old man are still here and anyone else who has joined their party, so we need to be careful. Keep your eyes peeled.'

Four columns later, we heard voices coming from the main cave area. The corridor was getting lighter the further we progressed, and the canyon breeze began to drift in.

'Almost there,' I whispered, edging further and further forward to the top of the corridor.

Erika was holding on to my shirt to keep us together. I held the gun out in front of me and was genuinely amazed at how quickly my close combat military training had kicked in. My head was scanning left to right, my eyes darting around the corridor as we approached the last column. We edged our way into the large cave.

As we stood against the damp wall, I could hear the old man and the chatty Russian talking to each other. I turned around to look at Erika, who had pulled out the Russian's mobile phone and placed it to her ear. 'I'm trying that number again,' she whispered, hoping that the mobile service would register now that we were closer to the exit.

The look of disappointment on her face said it all, and she closed the handset and placed it back into her pocket. 'We need to get outside.'

'Agreed. You wait here. I'll try to edge my way around the door.'

I dropped to my knees, crept past the last column and then up the small incline to the top of the entrance to the corridor. I leaned forward and turned my head to the right, edging just far enough out to be able to get a glimpse of the cave area with my left eye.

The large wooden doors were open, and a vehicle stood in the entrance.

The old man spoke loudly. 'What the hell is happening down there with those clowns? They should have killed those two and been back by now.'

The fucking bastard.

'Probably having some fun with the girl, yes?' the Russian replied.

'Well, we need to get fucking moving. Go tell them to finish the job and let's get out here,' he said as he lifted his phone to his ear.

The Russian did as he was told, pulled out his handgun from the holster around his waist and started to come towards the entrance of the corridor. He was almost on top of me and with no time to think, I launched myself up, raised my right arm, and pulled the trigger.

The bullet hit him in the throat and sent him hurtling backwards through the air. I ran back into the corridor and behind the first post, found Erika standing against the wall with the mobile phone open.

'It's him,' she said, pointing at the phone, 'Simmons, I got reception and told him what's happened. He said he knew where we were and that they were already on their way. How the hell did they know that?'

'We'll worry about that later,' I said. 'I've just shot another one, but we need to go now!' I was operating solely on adrenaline and now knew that the old man was the last one left and our only obstacle to freedom. I grabbed Erika's hand, and we rushed to the top of the corridor. I held out the gun in front of me and with Erika tucked in behind me, we made our way onward. The chatty Russian was on the floor, curled up in a ball, and the old man had disappeared. We edged forward, keeping our backs to the cave wall, and we were almost within touching distance of the vehicle when I heard his voice and saw his darkened shape crouched behind the large desk.

'I see I have underestimated you, Mr Davidson. Four highly trained operatives, and you still managed to get out of your cell. That is commendable.'

'Hold up the phone,' I whispered to Erika. I wanted to make sure the detective on the other end of the line heard our conversation.

'You lied to us, you son of a bitch,' I said, my voice echoing around the large open cave. 'I gave you the money, and you said your word was your bond. You could have walked away with the money and left us alone liked you promised.' All the while, I steered Erika slowly towards the armoured vehicle. I sensed what was coming. The old man was in a desperate situation.

'I couldn't leave a trail, Mr Davidson, you know that. You've seen the movies, that's not how this works.'

'You're a snake in the grass,' I said, shuffling ever nearer the vehicle, buying a little time.

'So what now, Mark? We stay here and just chat?'

'Why not?' I replied. 'We can just wait here until the police arrive.' I held up the phone so that he could see. 'They're listening to every word.'

No sooner had I finished the sentence than the old man snapped and went for his weapon. He was quick; it was out of the holster in a split second and he let loose as we dived for cover behind the vehicle.

It was time to deploy the big boy, and I pulled the machine gun from behind my back. I checked the magazine and flicked off the safety.

'Let's make a deal,' I shouted, turning on my knees to face the direction of his voice.

'What kind of deal would I possibly be interested in?'

'We just want to go home. You have the money and you know the police are on the way, yes?' I was stalling and hoped he'd take the bait. I looked up over the door and scanned the whole area. He was nowhere to be seen.

'Go on,' he replied.

'Here's the plan. We walk back to the corridor where we came from and you will stop firing your gun. Get in the car, drive away and leave us here for the police to find. We don't want to die and neither do you, so let's meet in the middle. You have what you came for, so take your chances and that way everybody lives to see another day.' As I was talking, I slowly raised my head above the rear of the vehicle again. I still couldn't see him.

I sat back down with my back to the vehicle door. Erika clung onto me like her life depended on it.

A voice. 'Okay, Mr Davidson, that's a good plan. The only way either of us will leave here alive, so let's do it, shall we?'

Could this be the way out of this disaster? I owed it to Erika. The last thing I wanted to do was to pitch her in the middle of a firefight. She'd go first. There was no way the old man would shoot her. Me perhaps, but not Erika, knowing that I was armed with a machine gun.

I whispered to Erika. 'Edge around the wall of the cave, crouch down, stay in the darkness and get back to the corridor. Got it? Don't look back, don't stop. It's only a few dozen steps and then you're hidden. I will finish the conversation and join you in a minute. Go as soon as I start talking, okay?'

She nodded at me and I turned again to face the desk area. I spoke. 'Okay, let's do it, Erika first and then me. Once we are both down the corridor, you can leave.'

'Agreed.'

Erika had made it.

Now it was my turn.

I moved, sweeping the machine gun from left to right. One step at a time, slowly and quietly, I stepped out until I reached the entrance to the corridor, where Erika suddenly grabbed me and pulled me into the darkness. She wrapped herself around me and we hugged in silence as we finally could see a small light at the end of this long, dangerous tunnel.

'I left the phone out there,' she said, 'in case we lost the mobile signal.'

'Good move. They'll ping the location and hopefully the entire Las Vegas Police Force will be on their way.'

I inched further back to the entrance of the corridor, raised my gun, and tried to stay alert. 'Okay, we have moved! Now it is your turn!'

But the old man was already there. I heard the door of the vehicle open and then slam shut. Within a second or two, the ignition fired into life and the vehicle started to move quickly as the wheels spun, sending dirt and stones back inside the cave as it launched itself forward.

We had made it. We had bloody well made it.

I grabbed Erika's hand, and we slowly inched out of the corridor and out of the cave. The vehicle was speeding off into the canyon and eventually disappeared in a huge cloud of dust.

A feeling of euphoria washed over me, and I dropped the weapon onto the ground. We embraced each other tightly and began to cry uncontrollably. We sobbed hard, euphoric in the knowledge that we'd just escaped a certain death.

We had witnessed sights that were inexplicable to normal, everyday folk such as ourselves. We had stumbled into a movie that even Hollywood would think was farfetched. The fear of loss, the fear of death, the fear of fear itself was completely overwhelming and only now, with the old man speeding off in the distance and our Russian tormentors lying dead, did it actually sink in that it was all over.

I held Erika's head against my chest, unable to control the tears.

'I can't believe it,' I managed to say, still sobbing, my body shivering.

'Me neither.'

Erika picked up the phone from the floor and wiped it clean. Incredibly, the detective was still on the line, listening in. 'They have our location!' Erika's face was beaming as she smiled the gorgeous smile that had made me love her so much. I was tired, emotionally, physically and mentally drained, but I knew the cavalry was on its way. On the grand scale of things, this was better than we had hoped for only a short time ago when death had stared us quite literally in the face.

53

Green light

'You have a green light. I repeat, you have a green light. We need to be in there right now!'

Simmons was screaming into the conference line at the teams. 'They have somehow managed to get out of the cave, but they don't know where the target is. He's in a vehicle.'

'We are five minutes out,' Bissett replied.

A ten second pause and then, 'Vehicle! Vehicle!'

'Bravo, report.'

'A speeding vehicle, sir, in the desert.'

'Intercept. I don't give a fuck what you do, but stop the vehicle and take him alive, do you hear me? Do it now.'

'Already closing in, sir.'

54

Respite

Clinging to each other, Erika and I made our way to the entrance of the cave and slumped into a heap in the doorway, gazing out into the vast canyon. The sun was setting in the distance and for the first time I could enjoy the peace and tranquillity of the Grand Canyon, in the presence of the woman I loved.

'Some holiday.' I placed my arm around her as she leaned into my shoulder.

'Some holiday.'

'I think we may need some serious counselling after this episode, that is, as long as I'm not sent to prison for murder.' I was staring out into the rocky canyon, my heart rate slowing down. It felt good.

'It wasn't easy. You were just reacting to the situation,' Erika replied. 'It was either us or them and luckily you got there first.'

She was right, of course, but I'd like to think it was more to do with British military training than luck. My mind drifted, remembering elements of the things that had just taken place and cringing at the thought of the dead bodies. 'But the money, the money's gone,' I added. 'He's taken everything, our lives and our dreams, all the plans that we'd made together.'

I guessed there was no chance of reversing the transfer. The accounts were untraceable. These men were professional. I hung my head between my legs, devastated at the realisation of what these people had done to our lives.

'Money isn't everything,' Erika replied. 'We are both alive, and we have to be thankful for that. I love you for who you are, not for the money in your bank or how big our house would have been. As long as we can be together, I really don't care about any of that.'

I held her tightly. I could not have been any happier to hear those words.

'I love you,' I said. 'You are right and I don't ever want to lose you.'

55

Approach

'Approaching the site now sir,' Bissett said, as the chopper slowed, heading towards the teams surrounding the cave.

'Every single eye on the cave,' said Simmons, 'We don't know who could be left in there, so proceed with caution and weapons at the ready. I've got the girl on the phone. According to her, all the tags are dead.'

56

A Haunting Sight

The noise in the distance, echoing around the vast openness, produced tears of elation as we looked up at the sky. A small black dot had appeared on the horizon, flying through the air in a straight line towards our cave.

Erika put the mobile phone to her ear. 'Please tell me that the helicopter flying towards the cave has something to do with you?' she asked frantically. She smiled slightly and looked at me. 'He says it's their team. We'll be out soon, thank God.'

I stood up, helped Erika to her feet, and placed my arm around her shoulder.

'It's time to go home,' I said, kissing the top of her head.

The chopper came closer and eventually hovered over the cave. The wind swirled and dust flew into the cave, whipping into our faces and bodies as we planted our heads towards the ground.

'We made it,' I whispered.

'Oh … oh my God,' she replied. Her head was frozen on my shoulder and her body had stiffened as she stared back into the cave. The helicopter was almost on the ground, blowing vast amounts of red dust and dirt straight towards us.

Confused, I turned my head to see what had made her so anxious. The last Russian I had shot and presumed dead, was lying on the ground, his AK47 machine gun pointing directly at us, blood streaming from the side of his neck. He was very much alive, and we stood motionless for a moment, staring at the lone gunman. We were completely unarmed and at his total mercy.

'Mr … Davidson,' he spurted, coughing up blood and spitting.

'Please,' I replied quickly, holding my left hand in the air, my right one wrapped tightly around Erika so she was behind me.

He managed to smile at me before coughing up another pool of blood. Coughing fiercely, his gun fell from his grip for a second and I could see no other option than to take immediate advantage of the situation and make a run for the helicopter.

I grabbed Erika's left hand. 'Run!' We ran for our lives in the chopper's direction. My whole life seemed to flash before me, images of my family, my friends, my childhood, the trip to Vegas, the helicopter ride that started this whole chain of events, the killings, every vivid memory sped through my mind before the unmistakable sound of a machine gun letting loose behind us brought me crashing back to a frightening reality.

I looked behind me and saw something that would haunt me for the rest of my life. The fear on Erika's face ripped through my heart. She looked at me as if to scream, 'Help me, please!'

Everything happened in slow motion as Erika's body jerked and then catapulted forward in front of me. She screamed out in pain as the bullets pounded into her. I stretched out both of my arms to catch her as she fell, her body limp crashing to the ground.

I froze. Her eyes were open, and she looked directly at me. A small trace of blood appeared at the corner of her mouth. She tried desperately to speak, but no words came.

I screamed as I picked her up. 'No, No! Please God … no!'

Armed men were now scrambling out of the helicopter, guns at the ready as I struggled towards them with Erika in my arms, praying that she was still alive.

Another burst of the machine gunfire behind me was the last thing I heard as I felt a sharp, hot sensation in the back of my head and then a jolting sensation as my body was catapulted forwards, sending the two of us to the canyon floor.

It was deadly quiet, and I found myself staring up at a dark sky covered with thousands of stars. I felt no pain, no emotion, no fear. Just a silent stare into the stars above me and a light-headedness that made me feel very tired.

Then I saw faces. The men from the choppers were huddled around me, their lips moving as they pointed in various directions, but they were moving slowly and I could not hear anything.

They were fading, the men in black outfits. A pretty blonde woman who looked vaguely familiar fussed over me. I felt an overwhelming urge to close my eyes and fall into a gentle, deep sleep.

57

Help

'Fuck. Sir, we have the couple, but they are badly hurt.' Bissett was rushing towards the two bodies. 'One of the tags was still active, sir. We've taken him out and all the others are down. Davidson and the girl are hit. Boarding them now.'

'Get them to Vegas Infirmary. We have the Tycoon's Number Three in custody with Bravo team.'

58

Rebooted

'Mark … Mark, can you hear me?'

I could make out a voice, but it was muffled and distant. There were shooting pains towards the back of my skull and with every heartbeat, the pain seemed to intensify. The noise surrounding me was getting louder and louder, as if someone had located a volume button and was cranking it up to the maximum.

My brain was conveying a message to my hand, telling it to move and rub the ache in my head, but it was glued to the spot and unable to move. My heavy eyelids began to flutter and slowly, my right eye opened. At first, I glimpsed a mixture of colour and extreme brightness, which made me close my eyes as the light sent a sharp pain to the back of my head.

'Can you hear me, Mark?

I tried to speak, but my mouth and throat were too dry and instead, my lips slowly cracked open a bit.

'Squeeze my hand if you can hear me.'

An overwhelming willingness to move my hand was making direct signals to my brain, to squeeze whoever it was standing over me, but I was stuck, unable to make any movement. The noise levels began to fade, the voices began to dwindle and as my eyelids became heavier, I heard the faint echo of a woman screaming out in the distance. 'Mark ... Mark ...'

Another voice was calling out, over and over and so loud that it hurt my eardrums.

'Squeeze my hand if you can hear me.'

Once again, I blinked my eyes. Slowly to begin with and then faster, trying to focus on my surroundings. My left hand squeezed in response this time, and I kept blinking, trying to adjust to the bright lights. I managed to focus on the left side of the room and as I squinted my eyes, a blonde-haired woman dressed in an oversized white coat came into view. She was hovering over me and squeezing my left hand. As I studied her for a moment and as her face came into focus, she smiled at me, squeezing my hand tightly.

'How are you feeling?' she whispered, letting go of my hand and writing something on a chart.

'Who … where … where am I?' My voice was husky and my throat was immensely dry. She held a cup with a straw to my mouth, and I drained the liquid through my chapped lips. My eyes started to adjust fully to the room, and I glanced from the centre to the right and then back to centre, taking in everything I could see, trying to make sense of where I was.

'You're in Ward 7 of the Sunrise Hospital in Nevada. Can you tell me the last thing you remember?'

I closed my eyes for a moment, but my mind was blank. 'Nevada?' I croaked.

'Yes. Nevada, Las Vegas,' she replied, looking at me with an odd expression. 'The doctor will be here in a few moments.' She gave me a smile and made some adjustments to a machine that I was hooked up to with a variety of wires and drips.

'Las Vegas?' I muttered to myself. 'How the hell?' I started to panic and tried to sit up.

'Please, calm down,' the nurse said as the heart rate monitor started to bleep.

'Calm down? How can I calm down? What the hell is going on here?' I was starting to freak out and my heart rate increased. The nurse pressed a red button above my bed and within seconds, two men came rushing into the room.

'He asked me where he was, and started to panic,' the nurse said.

'Calm down, Mr Davidson,' one man said. 'I'm Doctor Spencer. I'm going to give you something to help you relax.' A large syringe filled with a clear liquid was pumped directly into the drip attachment in my right hand.

'Please ... please ... what are you doing to me ... why am I ... '

As the words drifted, I felt a tingling sensation flow through my body. I stopped talking as the doctor fussed around me, checking the machine and then shining a small torch into both my eyes.

'That will help you relax, Mr Davidson,' he said. 'I'll give you half an hour and then come back to talk to you. Please don't worry. You're in safe hands.'

I closed my eyes and drifted away.

Doctor Spencer, dressed in a long blue overcoat, re-appeared in my room. He checked the machine and pulled up a chair next to my bed.

'Do you feel any better?' He sat down.

'I feel ... strange.'

'I'm going to ask you some questions. Now, please don't panic or try to put too much thought into any of it. If you don't know the answer, or it doesn't come to you straight away, just reply with a simple "I don't know", okay?'

He was in his late fifties, with thinning grey hair and tanned skin. He spoke with a deep southern accent and each word was very calm and precise. I nodded and took his advice, trying not to think too much.

'Before waking up, what is the last thing you can remember? Don't worry if you can't remember, just tell me your last thoughts before you woke up earlier.'

I closed my eyes and tried to visualise, but all I found was darkness. 'I can't … I don't …'

'It's okay, don't worry, let's just keep going. What is your name?'

'I …' I stopped and took a long, deep breath. How was it possible not to know your own name? I understood the question, but as I searched my brain for the answer, again all I could find was darkness. 'Someone has called me Mark, and you have called me Mr Davidson, so I guess my name is Mark Davidson.'

He sat forward in his chair and smiled at me.

'Excellent, Mark. I'm going to bring some people in later today to help us. They will attempt to explain everything that has happened to you. Please don't worry.' He patted me on the arm. 'You have been through quite an ordeal. You just need to be patient. You will have questions, but for now you need to rest.' He got up and tapped a pack of white liquid on the drip next to me. 'This will help you sleep for the next few hours.' He smiled, opened a small valve on the drip, and left the room.

I stared at the wall, unable to find any sort of meaning in the way I was feeling. How can it be possible to have no memories and no knowledge of who you are or any clue as to how or why you were in hospital rigged up to a large machine? How did I know where Las Vegas was yet I couldn't remember where I was yesterday? The thoughts drifted as my eyes felt heavy, and in a few seconds, I drifted back off into the darkness.

I was unsure how long I'd been asleep since the doctor left my room, but I felt surprisingly better than I did the last time I had opened my eyes. The back of my bed had been raised, allowing me to sit up slightly and take in my surroundings.

The room was quite large, yet I was the only person there. On the far left was another door. To my right was a small window and next to that was the main door leading out into the hospital. A small black TV was mounted on the wall and to the right of that was a white clock, showing the time to be 10:04 a.m.

I tried to inch further up in the bed but could only use my left hand. My right had a large drip attached to it.

'Hello, Mark,' a dark-haired nurse sang as she ambled into my room, breaking my train of thought. She checked the machine and then walked to the end of my bed, picking up a chart. 'How are you feeling?'

'Shit.'

'One of those is for pain relief,' she said, pointing to one of the bags on the drip machine. 'I've jumped you up a small level to help with the pain.'

'Why does it hurt so much?' I asked.

She smiled and passed me a cup of water. 'The doctor is due to see you very soon and he'll explain everything.'

'Please, tell me something. Anything. Tell me something about you.'

Her name was Pamela, she was 35-years old and lived with her dog, Dexter, in a place called Pioneer Park, Nevada. She told me she was five feet, nine inches tall, she had light blue eyes, and wore a size eight dress. She'd been practicing medicine for the past ten years and was now the senior nurse at the hospital. Her parents had died when she was very young and she had one sister who lived on the north side of Nevada, with her husband and young two children.

Then she hit me with a full list of favourites. Colour: yellow. Food: pasta. Time of year: Christmas. Music: Rock and Roll. Movie: anything old.

As I sat listening to her chatting away, I felt strange sensations after each sentence she had spoken. Yellow made me think of a yellow flower, but one I had no recollection of ever seeing. Pasta made me think of something the shape of a screw in a creamy sauce, but I had no recollection of ever eating it, how it smelt or how it tasted. Christmas made me think of snow and trees and that I liked it, I think, but I had no recollection of ever seeing trees or falling snow.

Every item she described, she would discuss. I could see it as clearly as a blank form but had no memory of ever experiencing them. As she finished telling me about a favourite bar, she frequented with friends on the weekend, the doctor walked into the room with two other individuals.

Pamela stood up from the chair and left as they surrounded my bed.

'Hello, again,' said Doctor Spencer. 'Great to see you sitting up. How do you feel?'

'I feel strange … I'm in a lot of pain and really confused.'

'I know, you will have lots of things circling around your head, but maybe it's best to tell you everything we know so far about your situation and what has actually happened to you. Let's see if it triggers anything. This is Doctor Samuel Bell. He is a psychiatrist here at the hospital.' Doctor Spencer pointed to a tall, thin man. 'And this is Agent Simmons, he is a liaison officer from your British Police.'

'Why is he here? Why am I here? What the hell is going on?'

'Doctor Bell is going to tell you everything we know so far. It's probably best you don't interrupt.

Just try to listen to what he tells you and try to focus on any memories that come into your head.'

The psychiatrist pulled out a file, opened it and began to read directly from it. 'We have you recorded as Mark Davidson, aged 34, from Newcastle upon Tyne, England. On Thursday 24th December 2009, you and a young lady, Miss Erika Johnson, boarded a private jet and flew direct from Newcastle International Airport to New York's JFK airport. You spent an evening at the Plaza Hotel before flying from New York to Las Vegas on Christmas Day. You then booked into the Bellagio Villas where you were due to stay for,' he paused to look at the script. 'Sixteen nights. Records show you reported a robbery three days later, where Simmons here took statements from each of you. We have copies here in the file. Do you recall that robbery?'

My brain was trying to process what he'd told me so far, but I was failing miserably. Private flights, New York, a robbery and Erika Johnson. What the fuck?

'Nothing,' I replied. 'None of that is familiar to me.'

'You reported a stolen blue diamond necklace. Bert Simmons left you his card and told you to contact him should—'

'A blue diamond necklace!' I loudly exclaimed. 'Wait, yes, I bought this, didn't I? Or did I?' Then it

289

was gone. Whatever that memory was, as quick as it had come to me, it was lost again.

'You purchased it for sure, and it was stolen from Erika's neck. Then we have you recorded on CCTV, inside a private hangar at Las Vegas airport. We interviewed a waitress who told us you and Erika were booked on a private charter helicopter which was due to fly you around Vegas and the Grand Canyon.

'Bob!' I shouted but had no idea why.

'Excuse me?' Simmons said, edging forward on his chair.

'I … Bob … I don't know. The name Bob came to me for some reason.'

I was so frustrated and wanted to scream at all of them. The inability to remember any of these events was simply incomprehensible.

'It's okay,' Doctor Spencer said. 'Let's just get through this and we can go back and re-visit parts of the story.'

'Well,' Doctor Bell continued, 'the helicopter that you and Erika hired for the day was found in the Nevada desert, completely burnt out. The captain was an undercover security agent and was found shot dead, his body dumped in the canyon.'

'What the hell?'

'And then Agent Simmons received a call on a cell phone from Erika and yourself, claiming you'd been kidnapped but had somehow managed to escape the clutches of some rather nasty characters. Simmons already had agents in the area and mobile units were close by, as was one of the police helicopters. As it was attempting to land, Erika and you were seen running from the entrance from an underground cave, but by the time the officers scrambled out of the choppers, an injured gunman had fired a machine gun at you and that's why you're here.'

My brain went into overdrive. Guns, helicopters, Erika. What the fuck was I into here?

Doctor Spencer took over from Doctor Bell. 'You were brought here with a bullet lodged inside your skull and one in your back. Without going into technical detail, the first bullet entered your back and damaged the nerves of your lumbar spine. This controls your legs, pelvis, bladder and bowels and removing the bullet was an extremely difficult and complex operation in itself. Due to the nature of the operation, you will notice you have very little or no movement at the moment but, Mark, rest assured, this is only temporary. The operation was a success and in the next day or so, with a little physiotherapy, you will start recovering.'

As he finished the first part of this conversation, and as if that was not enough to cope with, he seemed to shift his stance slightly, coming closer to me as his facial expression changed to look far more serious. 'The second bullet, however, is a lot more complicated. Let me explain the best way I can.'

'What is it?' I asked, 'Why are you looking at me like that?'

'It was lodged in the rear part of your skull.' He pointed at the back of his own head. 'Here. It was imperative we operate immediately and upon opening the skull, I was, well, a little surprised, to say the least.'

'Surprised?'

'Generally, if a bullet enters the brain, it can cause not only massive internal bleeding, brain swelling, and severe head trauma, but in most cases, will end in death. After opening your skull, we found a rather large growth underneath the brain tissue. The bullet had lodged in the growth and it was the reaction to this that made you pass out and not the actual bullet wound.'

'A growth? What do you mean, a growth?'

'Tests showed that you had quite a large tumour, and it was this tumour that inevitably saved your life, as it stopped the bullet from entering the main part of your brain. You are an extremely lucky man, Mr Davidson,' he added. 'You see, the tumour was actually quite large and I have no doubt it has started to affect your health. Small memory losses and blackouts are very common with this type of tumour and you would have experienced this in the past. Although the tumour growth was at the rear of your skull, it stretched along to the hippocampus part of your brain, which is where the cells were attached and that's where we have a slight issue.'

'Issue?'

'The hippocampus part of your brain is the part of the brain that affects memory. It's like a computer storage facility in here,' he said, tapping his temple. 'Every memory, every action, every thought becomes a memory and is stored away safely. When we opened up your skull to remove the bullet, we removed the tumour at the same time, but the tumour was feeding on the hippocampus. When the tumour was removed, we effectively rebooted the computer, or in layman's terms, we switched you off and waited for you to reboot yourself, which is exactly what you are doing now. You have actually been rebooting for some nineteen days now and should regain all of your memories over time, but this is rather a rare case and I'm afraid I have no clue as to how long this will take. Five minutes? One day, one week, one year? I really have no idea. Talking about events like this and talking to people you are familiar with, your family and your friends, may help the process.'

'Family?' I replied. 'I have brothers, don't I?'

He smiled at me, looked at the psychiatrist, and back at me.

'You certainly do, Mark. Two of them. They are here now, along with your parents. They are all very eager to see you, but I've warned them that you may not remember who they are and to not overwhelm you too much.'

'And the girl?' I asked, 'who is she and what happened to her?'

'She is in a coma and has been unresponsive to treatment. We have no choice but to wait and see if she can pull herself free. Her bullet wounds were far more extensive than yours and she was hurt badly. When you are feeling up to it, we will allow you to see her also, but right now your family wishes to see you and I think you've had enough information for now.'

He stood up and the other two followed and as they were about to leave, Simmons turned around. 'One last thing, Mark. Do you remember transferring two hundred and forty-five million pounds from your account to an account in the Cayman Islands?'

'What? What the hell are you talking about?'

'I thought not,' he said, 'but the doctor said you will remember eventually.' He placed his business card on the side unit. 'When you do, give me a call.'

My head was pounding. Kidnapping, shootings, a girlfriend, trips to Las Vegas and New York, two hundred and forty-five million Pounds? Who the hell was I and what the hell was going on?

59

No loose ends

For the past two weeks, the MI6 team had followed some of the Tycoon's tags to London and picked them up at Heathrow Airport. Interviews and interrogations had revealed very little, most of which they knew already.

Richard Thacker, the Tycoon's third in command, was the biggest scoop so far. After capturing him once he'd fled the cave in the Grand Canyon and in 40 hours of interrogations which were strictly 'off radar', he'd negotiated himself a swift deal and had given up some vital information for a more lenient sentence.

But Simmons and his direct team were still in Vegas. The Tycoon's Number Two was still in the city, which meant danger for Davidson and the girl. The organisation was not known for leaving loose ends, and these two were their biggest.

Caroline Bissett had taken up full-time residency at the hospital and was now acting as a nurse to stay close to Davidson. Another ten MI6 agents were in and around the hospital, around the clock. They had the hospital completely covered and local Vegas Police were present on every level.

Of course, they couldn't be sure if the tags would try anything at the hospital, but every measure was taken to make sure these two were safe and protected.

60

Familiar Faces

'Chris?' I asked.

'That's me, big brother,' he replied, smiling and tapping my hand. When I woke from yet another sleep, people who said they were my parents and brothers were now in the room and sitting around my bedside.

'Do you remember me?' my other brother asked, sitting forward and smiling at me.

'I think … I think I know your face. You're my brother, that's obvious because they told me I have two, but … sorry.' I felt dejected. 'They said it will come to me. In time.'

'I'm Andy. And don't worry.'

'Yes, don't worry.' It was my mother. Her eyes were red, she looked exhausted and was sitting on the very edge of her seat. She took my hand and I grabbed it and held it tightly. As soon as I touched her, it felt so right to have her next to me. I was overcome with an emotion that I struggled to understand and started to cry.

She jumped up from her chair and leaned into my chest, shaking.

A mixture of things started to circle my head: I remembered her in a kitchen, bending over me, rubbing my head and asking what was wrong after I'd collapsed on the floor. Then I was then riding my bike, and she was guiding me along the street, laughing as I'd managed for the first time to cycle fifty yards without my wheel stabilisers.

My emotions were in overdrive, and I could not stop the tears.

'Oh, Mark,' she cried, 'we're just so happy you're alive.'

'I know it's you, Mum. I remember things, little things but somewhere inside of me, I know that it's you.' I tried to compose myself as she lifted her head from my chest and sat back in her chair.

For the first time since I'd found myself lying in bed, I managed to lift my left hand, and wiped the tears from my eyes.

'We're here for you, son,' came a rather stern voice. The oldest man in the room, who was obviously my father, was sitting with his arms folded and looked slightly lost as to what to say, how to say it or, indeed, how to act.

I looked at him and, as with Andy, I tried to remember him clearly, but struggled to immediately generate a reaction like my mum. My brain was working overtime. 'The doctor said you should talk to me and fill me with information about my life, the past, happy memories and sad ones, whatever really that you think might help.'

For the next three hours and without so much as a break, the four closest members of my family began to enlighten me about a broad range of events in not only my life, but in those of the people around us and in the lives of the people around them.

It was mid-afternoon when the doctor arrived to ask them to give me a break and let me rest. I'd absorbed major amounts of information and it would be a good idea to allow the dust to settle.

My parents were staying as guests of the Bellagio Hotel manager, who had heard about the events and made the grand gesture to allow them to stay for free until this was over. They would go to the hotel for a few hours and return later that evening, prepared with more tales and recollections to fill my empty brain.

After they'd left, the emotional rollercoaster eventually came to a stop. I closed my eyes and tried to picture all the great memories I'd just learnt. I fell into another deep and eventful sleep. I was sprinting down a strange, dark corridor and in front of me was ...who? It was a blonde woman. That is all I could make out from behind her. I was following her further and further down what looked like a dark tunnel.

'Almost there,' she cried. 'Keep running, we're nearly at the end.'

We ran harder and faster, but the dark tunnel seemed to grow longer the more that we ran.

'It's no good,' I shouted, it's just too far.'

'No, it's not! Run faster, we've almost made it.'

Then she stopped running and stood perfectly still as I slowed down and stopped directly behind her. She smelt like flowers in the summer and as I reach out to turn her around, her body seemed to change shape. She turned around. Facing me was a colossal figure of a man who started chanting in a strange language.

He stepped backward and raised his arms towards me. He had a large black gun and pointed it straight at my head. He began to smile and then laugh in my face before his finger wrapped around the trigger.

'No!' I screamed,

'Mark ... Mark,' came a soft voice.

My eyes shot open. I held my breath as I scanned the room around me. I was in the hospital bed and

Pamela, the friendly nurse, was on my left. To my right was Doctor Bell, the hospital psychiatrist.

'A nightmare,' I gasped.

'It's understandable,' Doctor Bell said. 'The trauma your brain has suffered is pretty severe and as your memory returns, you will have strange dreams and visions which may make no sense to you, but more and more you will start and piece everything together.'

My heart rate began to settle and I used both hands to pull myself up slightly to get more comfortable. I looked at my legs and successfully wiggled my left foot, but unfortunately my right foot remained still.

'Patience, Mark,' said Pamela, fluffing my pillows to help me get comfortable. 'Just keep trying to move every now and then, maybe try to shock yourself into moving one foot and then quickly another. That might help a little. It's just a matter of time and it will all come back to you.'

She placed a fresh jug of water on the bedside table and left me to Doctor Bell for the next hour or so. We discussed my feelings and the memories that I'd recalled so far.

I'd recognised my mum and my brother Chris by name without them informing me. I had visions of achievements from my youth right up to adulthood and had recalled the person in my dream was actually the Russian thug who had shot me at the cave. It was like completing a jigsaw puzzle as my mind was opening and trying to fit all the pieces together.

Later, my parents returned, and we carried on with our reunion, talking about my childhood and trying to reminisce about as many joyful events as possible. We laughed together, which made me feel happy, although most of the time I did not recall the event and just laughed along in the moment.

They stayed for a few hours and were asked to leave somewhere near 7 p.m., promising to be back bright and early the next day. Nineteen days of uninterrupted sleep had wiped my memory clean and left me to work out the details for myself. From the sound of the events that had taken place prior to the shooting, I was partially glad that I didn't fully remember what had happened.

As I was lying alone, staring at the white ceiling, I thought about the girl, Erika. I thought it best to ask the nurse a few questions when I see her.

'What's happening to her?' I asked Pamela, who popped into my room to make up my bed for the evening.

She paused as she was tucking my new top sheet into the bed and let out a sigh. 'I'm not supposed to tell you things. The psychiatrist is supposed to do that, maybe speak to him tomorrow about it.'

'Please,' I replied, 'I don't remember her, but I feel like I should. If you can just tell me what you know, it might help me, please.'

She recorded a piece of information on my chart, closed my door slightly, and pulled a chair closer to my bed.

'Okay,' she whispered, smiling, 'but don't you tell anyone that I told you, you will get me into trouble.'

'Of course not,' I replied quietly. 'I would never do that.'

'She's in the room next door, here,' she said, pointing to the wall on which the TV is mounted. 'They brought her in with you, you were both in a really bad way. She was shot in the head, neck, and back. The doctors, well, they operated on her immediately and managed to remove all the bullets but …' She hesitated, her expression looked sad and she started shaking her head.

'What, but what? Please, keep going,' I said. I really needed to know what had happened now. I felt desperate, upset and angry, but still, nothing would register as to the reasons why.

'The bullet to the head was bad. When it entered her skull, fragments of bone followed the bullet into the brain. When they removed it, they also needed to remove quite a lot of pieces of skull too.' She shook her head slightly. 'She is in a coma and not responding to any treatment. The machine is keeping her alive for now, but no-one really knows if she will pull through. Her family is here every day, they're staying in the same hotel as yours. But it's been twenty days now and the longer it goes on, the more chance of permanent damage. Her brain is trying to repair itself, but the damage is just so severe … I'm so sorry, Mark.' She sat forward in her chair and took my hand. 'The physiotherapists are going to be working with you tomorrow,' she said, changing the subject, 'so when you're up and about, you can ask to go see her. Hopefully, by then you might have remembered something about her. I hope you do soon, I really do.'

She squeezed my hand, stood up, and moved the chair back against the wall. 'She has a brother, Tom. He keeps asking about you and wants to see you.'

'Tom!' I shouted as if a small light just went on in a part of my brain. 'I remember him, I think. But … but I can't quite make out his face. Where is he, is he here?'

'Her whole family is here, so yes, he has been visiting every day, too.'

'Please tell Tom I want him to come and see me.'

'It's difficult, Mark. I can't really imagine what they are going through watching her lying there, unable to do anything about it or even begin to understand why it happened.'

'Please, just ask Tom to come and see me.'

'I'll try.'

61

Closer

I slept for a few hours more and spent the rest of the early hours trying to move my feet and legs while throwing thoughts around in my head, desperately searching for answers to the ever-growing list of questions I had.

The doctor visited me early and informed me that the physiotherapist would be in today, to begin what would be a daily workout, until my brain figured out that I had legs and they actually worked.

I was flicking the TV channels once he left to see if I recognised anyone famous on the screen when I had a visitor.

'Hi, Dreamer,' he said, pulling up a chair.

I looked at him for a few seconds before I recognized him. 'Tom! It's you, I know you.'

'So you remember me then?' he asked, smiling and slapping my right arm.

'I know you Tom, and I know we are best friends, right? Did we put a bag of horse manure under the headmaster's desk and blame it on Dave Fisher?' I asked.

'About fourteen years ago, yeah, we did, and poor Dave Fisher was given detention for a week.'

'It's strange,' I said, 'just your face is helping me remember things from years ago, yet I can't tell when the last time was that I saw you.'

'Just before Christmas,' he said seriously. 'You and ... you and Erika were going on holiday and you picked her up from our house in a huge black limousine. Do you remember?'

Nothing. 'No. No, I don't. I wish I could, but it's just not there. They told me my brain is like a computer that is rebooting and now I have to wait for everything to kind of fix itself.'

'So you don't remember what happened? How Erika was shot and for what reason?'

His voice had broken slightly, and he was visibly upset and seemed to be trying not to be angry at the same time. His eyes were bloodshot, and he looked like he'd not slept in days.

'I'm sorry, I ... I'm trying, but right now it's just blank.'

306

Tom sat back in his chair and gave a long, drawn-out sigh as he pinched his eyes with his finger and thumb. 'I don't think Erika's gonna make it,' he said. 'She's just lying there and … we can't do anything. We talk to her all day, but we don't even know if she can hear us. Mum and Dad are there and they're convincing themselves that she will pull through and open her eyes and everything will be okay … but it's not, I know it.'

His voice broke, and he sat forward in his chair, put his head in his hands, and started weeping.

I sat in silence. I was unsure of what to say or how to react. 'I'm so sorry,' I finally said, reaching over and touching his arm. 'I feel so helpless lying here.'

'You're alive, Mark. Just be thankful for that. It will come back to you, I'm sure.'

'I know,' I replied, it's just so frustrating, when all the answers are in here.' I snapped, slapping the top of my head.

'You'll get there, mate.'

'I want to see her,' I said without thinking.

'Get your arse up out of this bed and you can,' he replied. 'Once they fix your legs. Have they said how long it will take?'

'Not a clue, the physiotherapist is coming to see me soon, so I guess I'll find out.'

Tom then bravely put Erika's condition aside and told me a bunch of stories that, although I could not remember, were rather amusing and undoubtedly helpful to both of us. We were clearly quite close and had been friends all the way through our childhood, going to school together, even sharing one or two girlfriends. We met every weekend with our good friends, Neil and Si, and had exactly the same taste in food, music and vodka. I enjoyed listening to Tom as my life seemed nice and simple in the real world, compared to the mess and chaos that had taken place recently.

We were interrupted by a nurse who arrived with the physiotherapist, predictably bang on time. Tom promised to keep popping in every now and again to see how I was progressing, and I assured him I would come and see him when I figured out how to use my legs.

The physiotherapist was a tall, stocky man in his late forties, called Rudy. He told me he would take no prisoners and that we'd be working hard and fast. We'd be working on mobility and he would massage my back and legs, working my tendons and muscles and getting me up and about using standing aids and walking sticks as fast as possible.

The two hours seemed like a lifetime as he prodded, poked and massaged me. I was up, down, legs in the air, bent backwards and then forwards, but, remarkably, I'd made positive progress. My right leg was now moving when I told it to, and so were my right arm and hand. My left leg was definitely weaker at the moment and would sometimes respond and sometimes just lay there, but my left arm and hand were moving great.

'More work tomorrow,' he said before he left. 'Don't go running away.'

'Fat chance,' I replied.

62

The Girl Next Door

Over the next few days, my parents and brothers visited, chatting more about my past. It was actually starting to work. On a handful of occasions, I had pre-empted their answers and the more we chatted, the more I was starting to remember.

Although Doctor Bell was pleased with my progress, he'd warned me to take things slow if I felt like too much information was entering my brain. 'You don't want to have a scenario where all of your memories come flooding back at once,' he said. 'Imagine your brain is a computer's hard drive and at the moment, you're processing one or two pages at a time. If you try to overload your memory, it's like trying to process thousands of pages at the same time. That could be okay, but also extremely dangerous, so take your time and keep resting.'

My dreams were making me happy. Memories from my childhood always seemed to be happy. My family was clearly an important part of my life and most of my memories were about them.

Two of my drips had been removed and although my head was still hurting, it was becoming a little more comfortable now that the tubes were out.

Tom was happy to see me up and about and pulled up a chair next to me.

'They found a tumour in my head,' I'd told him.

'A tumour?'

'Yeah, I know. I was shot in the back of my head and the bullet penetrated my skull. But I had a huge tumour growing inside my head and the bullet lodged itself straight in the middle of it. They say it's pretty rare and that they have never seen one like it here in Sunrise.'

Under normal circumstances, a tumour attached to your brain would not only terrify you but would be a life-changing event. But in the grand scheme of things, I'd cheated death several times and somehow the tumour didn't overly concern me.

'Did they remove it then?'

'Yeah, they removed the tumour and bullet together, but it was attached to some part of my brain that controls memory and that's why I'm forgetting shit.'

'Maybe it was a good job you were shot then, or they would never have found it.'

I never really thought about it that way and had read through the information that Doctor Spencer had left me. The tumour had grown rapidly and was graded at a Level 4, the highest grading. He'd told me I would need regular check-ups and brain scans in case cancerous cells had managed to split from the tumour and attack any healthy cells in my head.

I half-smiled at Tom. 'Never thought I would feel glad to be shot. I just hope it's done no permanent damage. If any cells from the tumour managed to travel I could be in for a rocky ride.'

Erika had made no progress, and they were now trialling her on a new drug, which had produced some success with unresponsive coma patients in London.

'I'm going to ask for a wheelchair and maybe pay Erika a visit tomorrow,' I said to Tom.

'Why not? It's good for her to hear new voices. The doctors have told us to keep talking to her and tell her about everything that's been happening. Some say she can hear us and it makes us feel better, you know?'

'Yeah, I know.'

My family was rather enjoying the luxury of the Bellagio and brought me some new toiletries from their bathroom on their next visit.

My brothers were bragging about a sizeable win they had at the casino, and it reminded me of the conversation with the agent a few days earlier. Two hundred and forty-five million Pounds, he'd said. Where the hell did two hundred and forty-five million pounds come from? And why did I transfer it to the Cayman Islands? It sounded like something from a movie. So many questions are unanswered.

After asking the nurse for an early shower, I was tucked into bed by 7 p.m., watching some random nature channel, when Tom popped back in to see me.

'We are going to the hotel to sleep tonight.'

'All of you?' I replied.

'Yeah, at least one of us has stayed overnight for three weeks now and the doctors have told us it could be a while before the new drugs begin to take effect. If they take effect.'

Tom was seriously down.

'Have some dinner together, have a good sleep and spend some time as a family. It's doing you no good staying here when you look like this.'

'Yeah, I know,' he sighed, 'it's just kind of hard to leave her, you know, when she's just lying there helpless.'

I barely managed twenty minutes of the nature documentary after Tom left. I lay in the dimly lit room, alone with my thoughts. Erika was the only thing on my mind.

I need to see her, I suddenly thought to myself. I won't leave her on her own for the whole night. I buzzed the nurse to my room.

Pamela was back on duty and jumped around the room in her usual jolly manner. She checked the machine as usual and made her daily note in my file, before jokingly asking what was so important that I needed to drag her away from the TV in the staff room.

'Do you have a wheelchair?' I asked.

'And why do you want a wheelchair?'

'Will you take me next door to see Erika? Just for five minutes, I just want to see her face and see if it triggers anything.'

'Can't you wait until tomorrow? I thought you were planning to go with her brother?'

'I will be, but she is alone tonight and maybe it's better that her parents and brother are not around the first time I see her.'

'Let me see what I can do,' she said as she left the room.

I had so many questions and I sat up in my bed just as Pamela came back with my very own wheelchair.

'You will get me into trouble,' she said as she parked it next to my bed.

The physiotherapist had actually worked wonders, and I could climb out of bed and into the chair on my own. 'I'll push the chair if you push my little machine,' I said, making Pamela chuckle as she followed behind me with the wired machine.

As I slowly moved out of the doorway, I glanced around the hospital for the first time. The corridor was pretty long to my left as I was in the last room at the end.

It was getting late. Thankfully, the hospital was quiet as I slowly made my way to the next room. My heart rate increased as I inched forward. I felt a slight apprehension as I approached the door.

'You okay?' Pamela asked when we stopped outside the room.

'I don't know, it's … strange. I know I want to see her and I know we spent a lot of time together, but something's missing.'

'Just take your time, okay, honey?'

I leaned forward in the wheelchair and pushed down the door handle, slowly edging it open. Slouching back in the chair, I took a long, deep breath and pushed the wheels forward as slowly as I could.

Her bed was raised higher than mine and I could not yet see her face. The bed position and the layout of the room were identical to mine, the only difference being the three separate machines that were bleeping away around her bed.

I rolled forward and parked the wheelchair next to the bed as Pamela placed my mobile heart machine next to me.

'Do you want me to help you?'

'It's okay, I just need a minute.' I closed my eyes and took a few deep breaths as Pamela secured the chair's brakes.

'Here goes nothing,' I said in a whisper, pulling myself up from the chair. Pamela stood close to me, just in case.

I stood for a moment to gain my balance, glancing at Erika's broken body in the bed. I looked at her face, which I could just make out from the corner of my eye. Another few deep breaths as I composed myself, trying to take it all in. There was no movement. She was lying still … sound asleep, the girl who had gone through the same ordeal as I had but hadn't been as lucky.

The first thing I noticed was her natural beauty. It actually took my breath away slightly. Short blonde hair, striking cheekbones, and such a pretty face.

A tear formed in my left eye but, peculiarly, I did not feel any deep emotion.

'Are you okay?' Pamela asked.

'I … yes, but it's … just odd.'

The signals were rushing around in my brain. My head hurt.

I turned to Pamela. 'Can you … would you be able to give me a moment?'

'I'll wait outside the door,' she whispered. 'Just five minutes, okay?'

The door closed, and I glanced back at Erika, lying unconscious in the bed.
The top blanket was wrapped around her and stopped just above her chest, and around her neck, she was wearing a shiny blue diamond necklace, which looked a little familiar.

'I've seen that before,' I said to myself as I slowly bent over the bed to get a closer look. More action was taking place inside my head.

She looked completely at peace, and I was thankful that she was not feeling any pain. I took her right hand and held it in mine as I glanced at her face, willing her to open her eyes.

'I … I think we are an item, you and I,' I whispered to her. 'Thing is, I can't remember you or us and I don't know what to do.' A tear rolled down my cheek and as I gazed at her, her face was becoming familiar. 'I know it's you when I look at you. I can't explain it, but I can feel my brain trying to piece it together.' I leaned over closer to her and touched her face, which felt soft and warm. 'I'm so sorry … for everything. You shouldn't be lying here like this. It's so unfair. Please wake up … I love you.'

As I uttered the words, I started to shake a little. I felt compelled to tell her how I felt. Then I felt myself falling. Letting go of her hand, I clenched my fists to my temples, wincing in pain. The piercing sensation shot through my head and into my eyes, like a bright light flashing into my pupils.

Pamela rushed back into the room and managed to catch me as my left leg gave way and I headed to the ground. I heard her calling for help and the pain in my head intensified, making me scream out loud. My vision was gone and the only sound I could hear was Pamela calling out. She'd managed to lay me on the ground as I clenched my head with both fists. There were more voices, but then it became quiet. I felt a sudden warm sensation around my body before darkness engulfed me.

I was sitting at the entrance to a cave with Erika, staring out into the Grand Canyon as two choppers approached us. It was the happiest I'd ever felt.

The dream lasted for days and had packed my subconscious with more memories than I was actually aware I had. When I eventually woke up, my parents and brothers were crowded around my bed, their faces showing great relief.

Doctor Spencer walked in to check up on me and it was my mum who spoke first. 'Mark, are you okay?'

'I … I think so, yeah,' I replied, rubbing my eyes and adjusting to my surroundings.

'They said you passed out.'

'Yeah, it was strange. I went next door to see Erika, just to, you know, try to kick-start my memory or see if I recognised her, and before I knew it, my head felt like it was going to explode. Memories that I didn't even know I had hit me and it was like, I don't know, like my head was getting overloaded.'

Doctor Spencer nodded his head. 'The brain is a very complex set of wiring and can handle a lot of what you throw at it, but thirty five years' worth of memories flooding back at once is an awful lot of information to process. It hit you hard.'

'I ... I remember everything, at least, I think I do. I don't know, really.'

'Oh, Mark.' My mum wiped her eyes.

'How long was I out for?

'Today is day six,' Doctor Spencer said.

'Six bloody days!' I exclaimed. 'I was asleep for six days?'

'Your body and your brain needed time to adjust,' he replied, 'but you have a really strong brain and clearly a strong will. You are a very lucky man to have come through this, believe me.'

I may be lucky to be alive and I may have a very strong brain, but I also remembered most of my memories from the past few months in vast detail. These memories included a full rundown from the day I won the lottery, the day I called Erika and asked for a date, the day we met and, of course, the day we were taken hostage by a madman and his thugs. They were painful and a part of me didn't want to relive them, but they did include Erika and how I felt about her, and I was happy for that.

The doctor left, and I told with my parents and brothers about the trip. They listened intently as I recalled the private jet and the trip to New York and our journey to Las Vegas. I did not tell them how I managed to pay for it.

'A private jet? That must have cost you a bloody fortune!' Andy exclaimed.

'That's another story.'

'Did you steal the money?' Chris was grinning.

'I won it.'

My dad spoke for the first time and looked at me with suspicion.

'Yeah, you told us you won the money at the casino, but the thing is … well, when I asked the hotel manager about the money, he had no recollection of it?'

'I … I won the lottery, Dad.' There was no point in lying any longer and I thought it best just to get it out in the open.

'The lottery?' asked Chris. 'How much?'

'Two hundred forty-five million Pounds.' I took a deep breath and braced myself for the reaction.

'How much?' Dad stood up. 'You won that much money and didn't say a word to anyone?'

'I'm sorry, Dad. The media was on the prowl, and I thought if I told everyone straight away, the world would find out and our lives would become a living hell.'

'It's already a living hell, Son!'

My mum and brothers sat in shock, unable to speak or move.

'I thought it would be best to just wait and let the media attention go away. This kind of money would have changed everything. You would have had media at the door, there would be beggars, thieves, conmen. Your life would have been turned upside down.'

'So that's why you were kidnapped?' Mum said.

'Yeah, they targeted me from day one. They must have had someone on the inside. If I had told you, you might have been pulled into this shitshow too. I have no regrets about not telling you.'

'Son of a bitch,' added Andy. 'All that money! Just think of the cars and women I could have had.'

'You're safe, Mark,' said Mum, always the voice of reason. 'You're safe and that's the main thing. The money doesn't matter.'

I gave them the full gory detail of everything that had happened in Las Vegas. Starting the story off lightly, I told them about the Villa and the fine restaurants we had visited. How we drank champagne and fine wine and had a great time. But then came the bad bits. I told them of the robbery and my ribs, which still ached, even now. I told them about the helicopter ride and how I'd planned the perfect day. A perfect day that changed the moment I watched the pilot take a bullet to the head. I told them details of what happened in the cave, that unless I transferred the money, we would be killed. But then my story changed course, and I told them we had no choice but to try to escape and that I had killed people in self-defence.

'Holy shit,' said Andy, 'you're James fucking Bond.'

As I explained every detail and emotion, they were stunned to learn the full extent of our ordeal and the look on their faces spoke volumes. Shocked was an understatement and as I finished recalling all the details of our romantic getaway, it was more like hearing a script from a movie. It made me feel extremely lucky to have come out of it alive.

My family stayed for a few more hours and then left me to rest, promising to be back later in the afternoon. My body was still in recovery mode and mixed with the drugs, I was feeling tired and groggy, which Doctor Spencer assured me was normal.

As I drifted back off to sleep, one memory that had lodged itself back into my brain was not only extremely frightening, but fired back all memories of the time in the cave. There was still one more thing that I needed to do that I'd not told them, for fear of the outcome.

'Wake up, you lazy sod,' I heard and felt a nudge in my right arm and slowly opened my eyes.

'Tom?' I replied, confused, rubbing my eyes.

I gave a rather exaggerated yawn and tried to pull myself up from the bed slightly to ease my comfort somewhat. Tom helped me adjust and passed another pillow behind my back so I was sitting up straight.

'Better, sir?

'Much. What time is it?'

'It's 11:20 p.m.'

'11:20 p.m.?'

'Yeah, your parents came back to see you, but you were completely out for the count. They stayed for a while, but the doctor told them you would probably sleep most of the day. They also came to see Erika, and we all sat together chatting for hours. It was quite nice actually.'

'That's good, will take their mind off things, I guess,' I replied.

'Anyway, I just came to check on you and see if anyone had told you the news?'

'Don't tell me you went to Vegas and won some dollars?'

'No, it's Erika,' he said, smiling. 'She woke up yesterday.'

63

Reunited

After an hour with Doctor Bell and my constant pleading, they agreed to let me see Erika later in the afternoon.

According to Tom, she had reacted well to the new drug treatment and was starting to show really positive signs. Although her condition was still serious, they had downgraded her status from critical to stable, which in itself was an incredible result.

But now she was awake, and this only heightened my concerns for her safety. I needed to see her.

Just after lunch, Doctor Spencer visited me and had kindly brought me a hospital laptop and telephone after I had requested these earlier in the day.

'Thirty minutes,' he said, leaving me with the devices. Panic was starting to set in, just like the panic I had felt in the cave and if I was going to settle my nerves, then I would need to act quickly.

Getting my wallet from the drawer, I located the business card I was looking for and dialled the number.

'Simmons.'

'Hi,' I whispered, 'this is Mark Davidson.'

'Hi, Mark, are you well? We were told you lapsed into a coma again and the doctors wouldn't let us near you.'

'Yeah, I'm recovering slowly. I was out cold for six days. But my memory is starting to come back so the doctors are upbeat.'

'That's good.'

'It's not good, I'm in danger,' I said. 'As soon as they find out my memory is good, and they will, they'll come after me, and Erika, too. She's awake as well, and we need protection. The man who stole my money, he vowed no matter what happened, he would kill us.'

'Mark, relax, we have it covered. The hospital is crawling with cops and we have one of our own people on the nursing staff. Besides, if they were going to try anything, then they would have done it by now, right?'

'Don't you get it,' I said, 'I'm awake. Erika is awake. They don't want us talking, they don't leave loose ends and we are huge ones, right? I don't feel safe. You're the only one I trust. Please can you come to the hospital yourself?'

'Of course, Mark. Of course. I will come and see you now, but rest assured we have the hospital completely surrounded by the good guys. They won't try anything. I'll be there as soon as I can.'

I'd thought long and hard about calling Simmons and putting my full trust in him, but felt it was safe as he had not only helped us during the necklace robbery, but had also stayed on the line with us during our kidnapping and had sent in the cavalry. If he was part of the old guy's gang, then I had no doubt we would be dead by now.

The doctor returned to collect his telephone and told me I could keep the laptop until the next day, so I could check my online banking and emails later. He also brought a wheelchair and a nurse, kindly informing me that I could see Erika for just a few minutes and then back to bed, as I still needed rest until the medication wore off.

I needed to see Erika, check that she was okay, and see if she knew who I was. My anxiety was through the roof, knowing the kidnappers could kick down our doors any minute. Maybe I was just being paranoid, and all they wanted was the money, but

I'd seen too many movies to know that gangs like this do not leave loose ends.

The nurse helped me into the wheelchair and pushed me out of my room towards Erika, with another nurse following close by with my heart monitor. As we approached her room, I became more apprehensive than at the first visit. This time she was conscious, and I was unsure how she would take to seeing me for the first time.

I gently opened the door and guided the chair into the room. Erika was slightly raised up in bed.

'Hi, Erika,' the nurse said, 'I've brought a visitor for you.'

Another deep breath and I pulled myself up from the chair and stood at the side of her bed. Her eyes were closed, a little colour had appeared in her cheeks and she had various tubes attached to her head and up her nose to help her breathe.

'Hey, it's me, it's Mark,' I whispered, leaning over the bed. 'I'm in the room next door and … just wanted to say hi.'

She slowly turned her head towards me and my heart almost skipped a beat as she opened her eyes and focused in my direction.

'Mark,' she said sluggishly, and even managed a faint smile. My heart melted.

'Hey, you,' I whispered, stroking her hair. 'I've missed you.'

Tears were streaming from my eyes, tears of elation at not only the sight of her but the fact that she remembered me.

'I ... I don't feel so good,' she said.

'It's okay, you're going to be fine. I won't let anything happen to you, do you hear me?' I was holding myself together as much as I possibly could. I didn't want her to see me upset. I held onto her hand tightly and for a moment, we just gazed into each other's eyes and smiled. It was amazing how much love I felt for her. At that moment, I would have done anything to take her pain away.

There was no way, as long as I had breath left inside of me, that this army of thugs would get to either of us without a fight. As long as I had breath in my body, they will not get away with what they have done to us. We'd come this far, and I was not about to let them finish the job they started.

'Let's be getting you back,' the nurse said. 'You have to take some medication, and this is as much as Erika can handle at the moment.'

'I need to go. I promise I'll be back soon.' I leaned over and kissed her again before sitting back in the wheelchair. I pushed myself back to my room and clambered back into bed, tired and exhausted.

The drugs were making me drift in and out of sleep and each time I managed to drop off, the dominant thoughts in my head were of Erika and the immense love I felt for her. But another thought kept interrupting the lovely ones: Where the hell was Simmons?

When I woke, I opened my laptop and logged onto my internet banking account, after getting the first password wrong twice. This would be the first time I would get to check my account balance since it had been emptied by my captors. It would at least allow me some closure to see what was left of the vast fortune.

I stared at my balance, looked up at the TV, and smiled. The old bastard had left me a few hundred thousand Pounds.

The hotel also had one hundred and eighty thousand dollars in winnings from our casino night, so at least all was not lost. That would be more than enough to buy a house and have plenty to live on for a while until we decided what we would do for the future. Finally, I logged into my email account and decided to pass the time by reading any new mail that had been sent since this whole episode began.

As I opened my mail account the door opened but I did not look up as I presumed it would be the nurse doing her hourly check. The door closed and as the person approached, I asked them to leave the door open, as it was quite warm and wanted a free flow of air tonight.

'I'm sorry' said the voice, which I instantly recognised. 'I just wanted to say hello.'

I paused and slowly lifted my head, quite shocked at hearing the familiar voice. 'Bob?' I said. 'What on earth?'

64

The Butler Comes Calling

'I'm sorry to call unannounced, sir, but I've only just heard what happened and jumped on the first plane. Are you okay?'

'I've been better,' I replied, still quite shocked to see him, especially at such a late hour.

'When I called the hotel to track you down, they told me what had happened and felt I needed to come and see if there was anything I could do for you.'

'I'm okay. I just can't believe you've flown all this way.'

'It's a terrible business, sir, and you were so good to me, it was the least I could do.'

'Well, I'm grateful, let me tell you.'

Bob looked serious. He asked a few more questions but not the sort of questions I expected. I put it down to jet lag as he walked towards my bed. 'Tell me, Mark, have you any idea who these people are?'

'Russians for sure, some sort of mafia.'

'They are like horseshit, Mark. They get everywhere, don't they?'

'I wouldn't know, really. I guess they're well financed, especially now that they stole all of my money.'

'Now, Mark. Play fair, we didn't take all of it, did we?'

My heart rate tripled in an instant. 'I don't understand.'

'This is what made you such a perfect target, Mark. Your innocence, your ignorance, surely you can see that it was just too easy.'

'What are you talking about, Bob?'

'The organisation was always destined to remove the great wealth you so easily acquired. And wow, were you an easy target, sir? You really were. I mean, hiring me as your assistant made everything so simple and meant I could track your every move.'

It took a few seconds to sink in. I was almost lost for words. 'You son of a bitch.'

'Now, now, Mark. Let's not get too personal about this.'

'Personal? Are you some sort of fucking idiot? I was kidnapped, my girlfriend was kidnapped, our dreams were ripped to shreds and you don't want to get personal?' I was so angry, I turned to face him, moving my legs out of the bed.

He reacted quickly. He reached behind his back and produced a handgun with a silencer attached, much like the one I had used back at the cave. Pointing it at me, he ordered me to move my legs back into the bed and keep perfectly still.

He had the upper hand. I had no choice but to comply. I swung my legs back onto the bed and felt a twinge in my ribcage. I did not take my eyes off him and he kept his gun pointed at me, watching me getting safely back into bed.

'Well done,' he said, patronising me and smiling to let me know he was in control.

'Have you people not ruined my life enough?' I asked, 'How could you do this to me? I trusted you and wanted to help you and this is how you repay me? You got the money, so what the hell are you doing back in my life?'

Keep him talking.

'You haven't worked it out yet?' he asked sarcastically. 'Well, let me enlighten you. I have been around for a long time and I have an unblemished record and a first class reputation in my field of work. Every job I am involved in is clean. No trace. No evidence. I am the most prolific cleaner you've ever seen.' He found this oddly amusing and laughed a little too long at his own jibe. 'So, the reason I'm here and back in your life, as you say, is to finish the job I started. I can't have you running around town telling everyone that you made it through this. Can you see how bad that looks for me?' He was almost apologetic, which made my blood boil.

Keep him talking, wait for an opportunity. 'The place is full of CCTV and police officers. There are witnesses who have seen you.'

'CCTV?' Tomorrow I will be out of the country, so CCTV really doesn't bother me.'

'You won't get away with this,' I said, looking furtively for something I could grab and hit him with. He was directly in front of me. He has started pacing the floor with the gun still held in his right hand. I had no options. Time was running out.

'Oh, but I will, Mark. I really will. The boys in blue won't be helping you either … let's just say they are no longer an issue. I will be long gone by the time they find both of your corpses.'

'So where is the money?'

'Long gone. It's been transferred and transferred and transferred, it's disappeared, the organisation are professionals, Mark.'

'So you were stealing the money for someone else? Are you just a tea boy or maybe a butler, just like you were for me? Does your boss tell you what to do just like I did?'

Maybe I had pushed things a little too far, as he stopped in his tracks and his expression turned dark.

'You listen to me and you listen well,' he said, walking round to the side of my bed. 'I will show you what sort of tea boy I am. I will show you exactly what I am capable of. You are just a small piece of dirt that is stuck in my shoe. When I finish my job, I remove the dirt so my shoes are clean.'

I had angered him, and he was ready to make his move. The bed's rail was lowered on my right and he stood there, gripping the gun. I sensed he was building himself up to a finale, and I had to get out. He gazed at me, smiled, and began to raise the gun.

At that precise moment, the door to my room opened and Pamela walked in. She froze when she saw the gun.

Bob turned towards her, pointed his gun at her head and told her to come in. This was my one and only chance. I grabbed the lowered rail of my bed and spun 180 degrees, bringing my legs sharply around in his direction with all of my might and launched myself directly at his torso.

As I landed on his back, the full force sent us both flying to the floor. He hit the ground with a thud as I landed on top of him. Pamela screamed and fell backward against the door. There was the unmistakable sound of a *phut* as he released a round from the gun. I watched in horror as the bullet hit her in the head, sending her body slamming against the door. She slumped to the floor, lifeless.

I had no time to think. I needed to react fast and in a split second I was on Bob's gun hand, trying to release his grip. But I was weak and my ribs were burning with enormous intensity. He was stronger than I was and I felt my strength draining from me as he slammed his fist into the side of my head.

The blow to the head shook me and everything seemed to happen in slow motion as I desperately tried to hold on to his body. I was clinging onto him as tightly as I could, but his right arm was still free and after a few seconds, he hit me again. The second blow was intense, and I released my grip and grabbed the side of my head. My ears were ringing, and the room spun as he started to stand up. One last chance. I swiped my left leg underneath him, catching him completely off guard, and he crashed to the ground. The gun bounced from his hand and slid underneath the bed. I threw myself towards it but he was almost on his feet. Before I could make any more progress, he got up, took a few steps towards me and kicked me full force in the ribcage. The pain was unbearable, and the wind was knocked out of me as I flew sideways, hurled into the far corner of the room.

As I glanced up, he pulled out a second, smaller gun. He pointed it at my face and managed a smile.

This was it. Game over. My heart sank as I slumped to the floor in defeat, still trying to wipe the blood from my face.

The doorhandle clicked again, and the door began to open. Bob took a quick step backwards, glancing at the door, but with his gun still trained on me. I was praying for reinforcements, but my heart sank again as a duty doctor walked into the room and stopped dead as the tray of medication crashed onto the floor.

With all my might and with everything I had left inside of me, I heaved myself towards Bob. He caught a glimpse of me from the corner of his eye and turned his head at the last second, and a deafening sound filled the air. The force lifted me off my feet and sent me crashing back towards the corner.

The pain was indescribable and my stomach felt like it was on fire as the bullet lodged itself into my intestines. I curled up into the foetal position, blood streaming from my midsection. I became quiet, knowing that my one and only chance was to play dead.

I lay perfectly still as Bob barked orders to the doctor.

'You, with me,' he demanded.

'Please don't kill me, I have young children, please …'

'Let's go. I couldn't give a fuck about your children.'

The room went eerily quiet, and after what seemed like a lifetime, I knew it was time to move.

66

Every Second Counts

It would be my only chance of trying to end this carnage. I needed to drag myself to the gun. I could have quite happily turned over and died, but the woman I loved was in the next room and a mad gunman was on his way to visit.

I eased onto my side, wincing in pain as the bullet burned my insides and my ribcage sent shooting pains down my spine. My head was numb and my body was covered in blood, which was seeping onto the floor, but nothing would stop me from trying to reach Erika while we still had a chance and I had a loaded weapon.

The pain intensified, and the blood continued to flow out of the fresh hole. If I didn't end this quickly,

I knew I would probably pass out due to the blood loss.

'You get out in that corridor and you stop that son of a bitch,' I told myself. 'The woman you love is helpless in the next room.'

I forced myself to painfully crawl under the bed, grabbed the fallen gun and hurled myself steadily past Pamela's limp body and approached the door. Quietly, I rose up and held the doorhandle with my free hand, took another breath and inched the door open fully. I placed my hand on the wound again to try and stem the bleeding, sending a sharp pain through my stomach. The burning pain from my stomach had me wincing and biting my teeth together, but my sheer determination to get to Erika was willing me forward.

I inched myself forwards to check the corridor for any sign of life. Bob was surely in Erika's room by now. Every second counted.

I heard voices coming from her room. I moved slowly and quietly out of the entrance, blood from my head and stomach leaving a trail on the floor behind me. As I approached the room, the doctor was standing stiff and still in the open doorway.

Bob was in his closing speech. 'You're the final loose end, young lady, so just give me that little necklace and then you can go for a nice long sleep.'

I stretched myself flat out on the floor. I inched forward until my head was almost level with the door frame of Erika's room and gently pulled myself behind the doctor so I could see what was going on.

Bob started to remove the necklace from around her neck. She had no energy for a fight. 'It's time to say goodnight, young lady,' he said as he reached for a pillow and buried the barrel of the gun into it.

'Please, God, no!' the doctor cried out, but Bob was completely focused on the job in hand as he lifted the pillow and the gun towards her.

I let out my breath, aimed the weapon at his head, and squeezed the trigger hard. There was the crash of a body falling to the floor and then darkness.

67

Simply Fate

'He's waking up,' a voice said.

The first sensation I had was the smell of sanitiser; the smell you would always associate with hospitals. The sensation was unmistakable and as I inhaled slowly, my eyes blinked. I tried to adjust to the light and my surroundings.

'Mark!' came the same voice to the left of me and I turned my head to find my mum sat at the side of my bed, my hand gripped tightly by both of hers.

Gently, I squeezed her hand and smiled at her, relieved to find her and the rest of my family around my bed.

'Oh, Mark,' she said again, 'are you okay? How do you feel?'

'Tired,' I managed to reply. I was completely exhausted, like I had not slept for days.

'The doctor said you lost so much blood that you might not recover.' I turned my head slightly to the right to look at my dad, who was speaking.

'Erika, where is she?'

Another voice. It was Doctor Spencer. 'Ah, Mark, you're awake. How are you feeling?'

'Erika, please, where is she?' The heart rate monitor beeped as my beats per minute shot up. 'Please, please tell me she's okay.'

'Erika is alive, Mark,' Doctor Spencer said. 'The bullet lodged in her stomach and, unfortunately, caused massive internal bleeding.'

My mum and dad stood and stared at me. They seemed lost for words. Oh no. The bastard shot her, I thought to myself.

'Where is she?'

'She is in our intensive care unit on the next floor. You will get to see her as soon as you are feeling up to it. Her family, and especially her brother, are asking after you, of course.'

I let go of my mum's hand, put both my hands over my face, and closed my eyes. Suddenly, it felt as if my head exploded with rage. A fierce hatred for Bob and the Russian gunmen, the men behind the plot who had been quite prepared to kill us in cold blood, swept me up. I let out a long, chilling wail. I felt hands on me, hands from the people I loved. I heard Mum sobbing as hard as I was, and then I felt something in my arm. The doctor had sedated me and, in a way, I was glad because I knew it would bring me peace.

It was the fear of losing the woman I loved that drove me to kill. I regretted nothing. Wave after wave of emotion washed over me and then, once again, darkness.

When I awoke, there was nobody there, and I felt desperately alone.

I needed to be with Erika.

Doctor Spencer returned soon after and we talked for a short while. He told me about the armed guards who were outside and how the police and Simmons and his team had searched the hospital and they were sure that there were no other gang members around.

I drank water and nibbled on hot toast, not really caring for my own well-being. I could not get Erika out of my mind.

A nurse brought some medication and my parents and brothers visited briefly.

When Doctor Spencer came to check on me, I begged him to let me see Erika.

'Mark, you have lost over half the blood in your body and were only moments from death. I know you need to see her and I promise you, when you are strong enough, I will personally take you to her. But for now, you need to rest and you need to get your strength back. You need to sleep.'

Sleep was the last thing on my mind. I needed a distraction, at the very least. Trying to take my mind off things, I looked around the room and found a pile of my unread emails that I'd asked to be printed.

There was a heap of emails from my bank, confirming payments that had been made throughout my visit to Las Vegas, and confirming that I'd successfully transferred two hundred and forty-five million pounds to a numbered account in the Cayman Islands. I wasn't dreaming. That nightmare had really happened. I picked up another email.

'Dear Mark,

Firstly, I would like to personally thank you for investing in my business. As discussed, I have utilised your funds to allow production of the chips and have successfully completed the initial stage. We have meetings with potential bidders on the mass manufacturing of the chip, so I just wanted to drop you a quick note to thank you again and any further advance. I will, of course, let you know.

Regards and best wishes, James.'

I put the email down on the bed and looked up at the wall. 'Of course,' I said to myself, 'the golf chip …

good old James.' I had completely forgotten about my big investment. It had paled into insignificance during the events that had taken place since that contract had been signed.

I smiled as I picked up another mail, dated a week later. It was also James.

'Mark. Hope you're well, just sending you a quick mail to let you know that I've tried to call you a few times and need to speak with you quite urgently. If you could give me a call as soon as possible, I believe it would be of benefit to both of us. Regards, James.'

I put the email down and started to drift off as fatigue and the natural healing process took over. James could wait. My only priority was seeing Erika. Knowing my bad luck, he'd be telling me that my investment had gone down the drain.

I slept on and off for another two days. I was conscious of staff telling me that Erika and I were making good progress and that she had been moved out of intensive care.

I asked to see her again.

'Soon,' the doctor said.

Fuck! This was so frustrating.

The hospital had been great, though. I had no complaints and looking on my bedside cabinet I noticed another small pile of printed emails and a few magazines. They were doing all they could to keep me distracted.

I reached over and picked up an email that looked as if it had a document paper-clipped to it. It was dated yesterday.

Hi Mark,

I have tried to contact you on several occasions and eventually got hold of your legal representative in the UK. (Si.) I'm so sorry to hear about your experiences and I wish you all of my best for a speedy recovery.

Sorry to get straight to business, but I'm afraid we are on a very tight schedule and we have 72 hours to read the documents (Attached) and come back with an answer

I have sent your legal counsel a copy of this email and asked that he read the legal documentation attached and confirm all is good to go. Once you've read this, you will need to call me to finalise the details. The chip has generated quite a lot of interest from the golfing world and after a few successful meetings; the word started to spread.

Within days, we were inundated with calls from pretty much every major manufacturer in the golfing world. To cut a long story short, the CEO of Acom Ltd, the biggest and most cash rich microchip manufacturing company on the planet have made us an offer. Basically, they want ownership and want us to walk away and allow them to mass produce and sell the product as their own brand.

Normally I would be against this, this is what happened the first time. However, that was until I read the offer. Please make sure you are sitting down when you read on because when I read it, I nearly fainted.

*They have offered us $900 million. Your 49% share of
the company would entitle you to $441million. Not bad for
a small investment of $5 million wouldn't you agree?*
*We have much to discuss and we need to move fast, but I
think I know what you will say. $$$$$$$$$$$$$$$$$$$$* ☺
*I've attached the documents for you to read, so please
call me and call your legal guys and let's get this deal done
so we can celebrate.*

The bubbly is on ice, buddy.
James

Just as I finished reading the email, the door
opened, and the nurse walked in.

'Get me a phone please,' I asked. 'I need a phone
now, right this minute.'

She put her hands on her hips and let out a sigh.
'Well sure, Mark. If that's what you really want, but
I've been sent downstairs to take you up to see
Erika.'

'I ... '

'Yes?'

'The phone can wait,' I said. 'Get me a bloody
wheelchair, now!'

Simply Fate – Retribution

Part 2 of the

Simply Fate Trilogy

coming soon

Printed in Great Britain
by Amazon